HYSSOP

HYSSOP

KEVIN McILVOY

 TRIQUARTERLY BOOKS
NORTHWESTERN UNIVERSITY PRESS
EVANSTON, ILLINOIS

TriQuarterly Books
Northwestern University Press
Evanston, Illinois 60208-4210

Printed in the United States of America

ISBN 0-8101-5085-9

Library of Congress Cataloging-in-Publication Data

McIlvoy, Kevin, 1953–
    Hyssop / Kevin McIlvoy.
      p. cm.
    ISBN 0-8101-5085-9
    I. Title.
    PS3563.C369H97 1998
    813'.54—dc21   98-8392
                                      CIP

For Fr. Art Robert,
grace & flame

Thou shalt sprinkle me,
O Lord,
with hyssop,
and I shall be cleansed:
Thou shalt wash me,
and I shall be made
whiter than snow.

Psalms 51:7

The author gratefully acknowledges the magazines that first published sections of this novel in slightly different form:

Blue Mesa Review, 8: "Hyssop"
The Chariton Review, 20, no. 2: "Eusebio's Christmas Trees"
Ploughshares, 22, no. 4: "Green House"
TriQuarterly, 97 (Fall 1996): "Portrait of Pancho Villa's Lieutenant, Manuel Hernández Galván, Shooting a Peso at Fifty Paces"

For their encouragement now and ever, the author acknowledges Colin and Paddy, Margee, Wendell, and Martha McIlvoy, Dan Ursini, Ellen Bryant Voigt, Reg Gibbons, Rick Russo, Nat Sobel, Robert Boswell, Antonya Nelson, Chris Burnham, Ann Rohovec, Leslie Coutant, Stuart Brown, Jane Abreu, Kay Byrd, Louise Gore, Theresa Gerend, Mireille Marokvia, Chris Hale, Romelia Enriquez, Tom Hoeksema, Paula Moore, Rita Popp, A. M. Mackler, Arthur Pike, Rhonda Steele, Jim Earley, Greg Romer, Don Kurtz, Kent Jacobs and Sallie Ritter, Pete Turchi, and Reed Dasenbrock.

HYSSOP

It is one lucky eighty-seven-year-old jackass whose jailer is his confessor. If Las Almas did not have its own jail I would be in the Dona Ana County Detention Center and would have no one to tell the stories to, that I used to tell in the confessional.

Cleophas Galván, son of Pancho Villa's lieutenant, Manuel Hernández Galván, has his right hand resting low on my waist and his left hand in my hand, and we are practicing the dance lesson he has just received from my wife Recita. I am humming "Blue Eyes Crying in the Rain," and sometimes singing a part that I remember or the parts of "Always on My Mind" that I mix it up with.

Recita is allowed to visit me here every day because Cleophas, who will marry soon, needs her to come and show him the steps. Though I have been in jail many times, I am never in for long, so he and I must make the most of our time together.

I hum-sing, "Other arms reach out to me, hmmm hmmm smile tenderly." He should lower his hand on my waist. He should press. He should almost rest it on my hip. He should touch lightly. He should lead. "Like this—like this," I tell him. He should gently let his hand roam to the center of my back and then lower, and then back again to my hip. But he must not be annoying. He must not spread his fingers. He must not mash my hand in his hand. When I tell him this, he says, "Red, I'm embarrassed."

I answer, "You're beautiful when you blush," and bat my eyes. He stops. He stamps his boots, handsome ostrich-skin boots, to knock the shame off him. Then, he takes my hand, my waist. We begin. Who would guess men like us ever could or ever can tell what they know—or ever will listen to each other if they do?

This—this compassionate arrangement—compassionate for me, compassionate for Cleophas, and for my wife Recita— this has been the plan of God and of Judge Isidro Mérida, nephew of my grade-school teacher Sister María Josefa, a terrible angel of our Mesilla valley, who still appears in whirlwinds on the dusty playgrounds of our schools.

I ask Cleophas if he wants to know a story about his father.

"No," he says.

"About yourself?"

"No."

"About me?"

Cleophas says, "They're *all* about you. You tell stories like a coyote spitting up his own bones, Red. And who can put them together?"

"Like this—like this," I say, and leave less space between our legs and waists. "Intimate. Be intimate." I wipe my leaking nose.

"Okay," he whines.

I lead, of course.

I have always one story in mind and others that interfere. I am like the mulberry on the *malpaís* where once my friend

4

Frank threw junk into the limbs night after night. When the nest of junk in a tree is large enough, there is more nest than tree. What kind of story is that?

My mother was from Matamoros. My father was American Bottomlands Irish, "knocked from the nest of Sligo jailbirds," he said. My wife Cecilia was born and raised in Las Almas, like me, though her parents were a Kraków Polish woman and a Tijuana man.

When I was born here in Las Almas, New Mexico, in 1909, I was not dark. I was not white. I was red, the brown-red of a dirty hammered thumb. I was red and, so, I was called Red. This is my history I trace my hand along.

My mother and father. Ana and Charles. They were both of the One True Faith. Catholicism, I mean. And so I had a Christian name, which was William Butler Alonzo Narvaes Greet, not half as right as Red. People ask me, Red, where did you learn to talk that way? All that salt and spit and incense? I learned from Our Mother Church's Latin and Her chapter and verse. I learned from the music of my parents' voices, which flowed from the seas and rivers they grew up within the sound of: the Shannon, the Atlantic, the Río Bravo del Norte, the Gulf of Mexico.

I was loved. I was raised beneath and grew straight from that good slanted light. I tell you, in the darkest time, the terror time, the heat of it reaches into me still. I was loved.

And how do I know I was loved?

My parents showed me. In her purse, my mother kept a folded piece of paper, and my father had one like it in his wallet. The paper was finer than onion skin. *Papel de chine,* they called the paper.

On my birthdays, and all my adult birthdays, they unfolded these papers and showed me. The first day of my life they had traced my feet, and they showed me them.

My heart is smaller now that my parents are gone, and now that my dear Cecilia, who did not ever ask to hear my sins, has died.

EUSEBIO'S CHRISTMAS TREES

On the gate of the Christ Is King church cemetery Eusebio put up a sign. Eusebio's Christmas Trees. He had a flashlight lighting it up, and I could follow that glow across the distance between me and everyone, the living and the dead.

I did not ever say, "This is a cemetery, Eusebio, you should not sell Christmas trees in this sacred place." All of us in the parish knew that behind him were his nephew, stepsister, and her husband, in their graves, gone a long time ago from this world's sacredness and sinfulness. We did not know how they died. Did we?

I've got my own notions anyway that some have more claim on the dead than others. The morticians in our valley are Catholics, and they have their way with the Catholic dead, so we are buried with our hands folded in prayer. Eusebio's brother-in-law, who may never have prayed in life, has prayed without cease since death, and Eusebio's dead stepsister, who may have prayed one rosary each day, now prays many. The child, Eusebio's nephew, was only an infant. Who can know what he prays?

Eusebio's business operated like mine. Like robbery. Yes, I'm admitting this to you. But then everyone in my parish already knows my record, the whole long eighty-year chain. I learn what people have. I find a way to take it.

Eusebio had never sold trees before. He owned a motel, Eusebio's Motor Inn, out on Picacho Avenue, a two-story success story. And now, a Christmas tree business.

Getting into their cars after church, people looked over at Eusebio's sign and at him. That Eusebio, they said. Loco.

Warming up their engines: Looks like he doesn't have many.

Turning on their car heaters: No. Not many.

And driving away: Wonder how much they cost?

That was the first night of the first week of Advent in 1994. The ironwork in the gate to the cemetery had been made by some guy in Santa Fe, very artsy, you know what I mean. A blooming cholla cactus raising its six or seven iron arms to fly, right here in Las Almas. We saw Eusebio's sign, and we started on our way, bearing our checkbooks, our cash that should have gone into the collection basket. He opened one side of the gate and brought us inside the darkness, closing that flying cactus behind us. He was respectful-like and solemn.

He didn't have many, oh, maybe a dozen. He had different sizes, with different problems. Every one had a price tag, and every one was the same price: fourteen bucks. People asked him were they Scotch pines.

"Mexican," Eusebio said, and who would not believe him? They leaned out of the fencepost holes the way the people lean who throw their hearts like nets across the border. If it was green on the outside, brown inside, the tree was—you'll say I'm lying, but it was, it was—beautiful. With crunched limbs, or almost no trunk at the bottom, the tree was irresistible. With no tip like a Christmas tree should have, the tree was unique. I can't explain. The darkness maybe. And the people had just come from Mass, you know, where they'd gotten some motivation: "There will be signs" and all that.

I watched this at first because I like to watch people's methods, people's own Masses that they celebrate, and then because I have always liked a Bible kind of a story that adds on and keeps adding. One beatitude, one blind man healed does not interest me. I like a story with many plagues and punishments, with one begatting leading to another. With more than one miracle.

In Advent we have an evergreen wreath we make, we Catholics, and it has three purple candles and a rose-colored one in its branches. Each week during the four weeks of Advent our priests light one more, saving the rose one for the third week. You'll have to ask a better Catholic than me why we don't start with the rose one. But you get the idea: a little more light coming into the world each week until Christmas, when the wreath has one white candle in the middle of the others. People say, "Look. Light. So much light." And the second week they say, "I'll be damned. More light. What could it mean? It could mean something."

Next to me in the pew, close next to me every Mass, was Recita Holguín, who knew everything about everyone in our church. This was her way, to be very close to people, close enough to smell of you. Her, she smelled like buttered cornbread. She was eighty-four. I was eighty-five. During Mass I had some imagined encounters with her. A handful, no more.

Not many more.

I imagined she held herself against me, her palms pressed into my chest, and recited my name: "Red Greet. Red Greet."

"Here?" I whispered. "In the church?" My nose trickled. I have a nose rag I carry, a white cloth napkin I stole from Gamboa's Restaurant. I have three, and I am sorry, God knows.

I imagined Recita couldn't help herself, dear Recita, who

10

sang to me, "Thou who didst bind and blend in one the glistening morn and evening pale," so close to my ear her singing made my hair moist. I touched her fingers with my fingers, spreading them to trace the softest parts. "May we knock at heaven's door?" Recita sang.

Why confess all this that I only imagined, why use her name and mine?

All my storytelling is selfish. Why pretend it isn't?

I could have moved away from her in the church pew. I sat there thinking I could. But I couldn't. My wife had abandoned me. 1972. She abandoned me. I don't know how else to say that she slowly disappeared in her bed, resentfully wanting no connection between us.

Burning with shame, I stayed near Recita. Christ, have mercy on me. Only her purse was between us in the pew. If I nudged it, it clinked. We said the prayers and we sang like two rough stones in a tumbler.

We all, all of the Advent People, the people in waiting, find hope. Then, trust. Dumb old candles, paganlike rituals. When the third Advent candle gets lit, something in the darkness is almost completely brought into the light.

What is it people feel? Ashamed is my guess. But hopeful. Trusting. And then we feel surprised—by what? By hoping! Trusting! All the poor Catholics who have nothing are surprised by all they've got. The rich Catholics who have it all are surprised to find they have only as much hope as the poor. On Christmas when that white candle is lit with all the purple ones and the rose one dancing flames around it, the people in the church are burning. You feel lifted up, the way a flame barely lifts itself up and wavers.

Eusebio sold all his trees. Each night of the first week of Advent he sold out. He let me sit with him at the cemetery gates. A kindness. Eusebio was an important man in Las

Almas, though only the breath of the Holy Spirit had raised him from the dust. He would tell you, too easily and with too little shame, that his mother was the descendant of Bernardo Gruber, peddler of tin grails, who once sold people folded strips of paper that had been smeared with the honey of Fuenteabejuna in Spain. The place of the Bee Well. If you chewed and swallowed this paper, very pricey of course, you would be Encantado, Maravillado, Invulnerable. Inflamed, Enchanted, Invulnerable for one day and one night. These papers were the first lottery tickets—in the 1670s! Soldiers bought them from Señor Gruber. And people who were called before the Inquisitors had bought more than one if they could; and the Inquisitors themselves owned many. The wounded and diseased carried the paper strips with them in preparation for the Day and the Time. They were given as wedding gifts. Priests bought them from Señor Gruber and blessed them and resold them at the higher ecclesiastical rate.

He knew I was a thief, but he must have believed I was harmless despite everything he knew. He did not let me make change because I am not *that* harmless, everyone knows. Though I didn't see him counting all the money wadded up in his trouser pockets, in my mind I counted bills for him, putting the faces up and smoothing them out. Washington. Lincoln. Hamilton. Three piles.

I heard the people ask him, "Where do your trees come from, Eusebio?"

"From very near," he said. He could have meant Mexico.

"Where do you find them?" the people asked.

"From very far," he said, which could also mean Mexico.

We asked, "Who brings them to you?"

"Who?" he asked back.

"Eusebio." I looked at his eyes and his long, wolfish muzzle. "Is your hearing aid working?" He had an ancient pink one sticking out of his right ear like a cooked shrimp.

"Huh?" he answered. He was having his fun. This hearing aid of his had a plus and a minus sign marked on it. You could see them when you were talking to him, but only he knew where the dial was set. Eusebio was a prosperous businessman, the owner of a motel, his hair and beard trimmed, his winter pants dark wool, dry-cleaned. Wrinkles had settled in him but they would not settle on him. A man like this can kneel right next to us in our churches, next to but not along with all of us, do you see?

I repair the walls my father once built all over this valley. And I am a caretaker. Yes, I am a thief. But I am a caretaker for churches and for rich people's homes, this is the work that I have done for almost sixty years. I do not steal from the people who hire me as a caretaker. I do not steal much. My stealing has always been venial sin and not mortal sin. I have often been fired. I have been caretaker for mayors, bankers, doctors, professors, and I have become their friend. Or their enemy. I have not retired from caretaking, why should I? I am good at it.

One evening in Advent I heard someone ask Eusebio why I was with him, whether he had used good judgment in choosing me as a business partner.

Eusebio shrugged. I saw him offer the man, Mr. Holy-in-the-Front-Pew, only that much answer, instead of saying, "Red is not with me. Red is not my partner."

I took it for friendship, this shrug. Was I wrong? Didn't Eusebio recognize my friendship? My natural generosity? We had known each other since Catholic grade school. Standing in circles with other children, we had played games with the girls on the playground. We had sung:

Agua y té,
Matarile rile rile
Agua y té,
Matarile rile rile ron.

¿Qué quiere usted?
Matarile rile rile
¿Que quiere usted?
Matarile rile rile ron.

Now I built a bridge of answers and questions I might offer to Eusebio: *You should be my friend, after all, Eusebio. Shouldn't you? I've kept you company here, I've guarded your interests, haven't I? I'm helpful. Blessed is he who comes in the name of the Lord. Have I been helpful? I have, it's plain. Have I been loyal? Amen.*

I built my bridge across the distance between us, and when I had crossed it, I felt I was a business partner, of course I was. Why hadn't Eusebio told Mr. Holy-in-the-Front-Pew how proud he was to be Red's partner? My love for Eusebio and anger toward him made me stay there with him night after night.

At about eleven at night on Sunday in the second week of Advent, Eusebio sold a scrawny, uniquely beautiful, irresistible tree to my best friend, the Bishop, Francisco Velasco. Already the Bishop embraced the tree. He kind of fox-trotted it out of its fencepost hole, and poked his head around its thinnest branches to ask, "This is fourteen?" I loved this man. Eighty years I loved this man. He was an angel, the Bishop. Here is how you know an angel when you see one: the real thing, a living-on-earth angel is always amazed. "This is fourteen?" he asked, amazed that one Hamilton and four Washingtons could buy something so priceless. The Bishop greeted you this way: "Red!" It was like he was saying, "Red! You're still alive! Red! You're out of jail!" If you could answer back, that amazed him; if you shook his hand, he shook yours back as if you were Lazarus. "Red! Red!"

In the confessional I liked to confess my sins to the Bishop. A good lie delighted him, even a lame one. I confessed—again—who knows how many times I made the same confession?—I confessed the sin I've lugged everywhere and all over, the whole long chain of stealing. It is very foolish to carry such a thing, so tiring. But I do not know how to stop.

My wife Cecilia, I blamed her. My mother, the healer who could heal Cecilia's anger but not her body: I blamed her. My need, I blamed that, my need to have what everyone else had: life now, not still-to-come, life unalone.

When I finished my confession, he said, "Red!" We both laughed because, you know, it's the confessional, there is this window made of caning between you, and you're supposed to be pretending the priest is God and God's supposed to be pretending He doesn't care who you are. Then, the Bishop forgave my sins and asked me not to sin again. "Do you think you can do that?" he asked.

When I was a boy, the priests would use the Latin words for forgiveness: "*Misereatur tuin omnipotens Deus, et dimissis peccatis tuis, perducat te ad vitam aeternam. Amen.*" The sacrament of confession, the other sacraments, and the Mass were all a veil of words drawn across understanding or meaning, so what you almost thought you knew you never really could be sure about. I mean, you were at the mercy of your faith. I think the Latin meant that God is miserable sometimes too, and it's all okay with Him even if you keep doing it *vitam aeternam,* the rest of your life.

The Bishop said goodnight. I mean he said, "Goodnight!" His home was on Harding Street, east of the cemetery. He carried his tree through the cemetery gardens, unafraid of all the contrite Catholic spirits, guiding his green partner around the ribs of the white fences and past the goliath statue of La Virgen de Guadalupe. The back of his red and orange jacket had *Albertson's The Superstore!* in Superman lettering across it.

15

When the Bishop was only another fold of darkness at the far end of the cemetery, I said, "I love the man, don't ask me why."

"Yes," said Eusebio, taking my arm, leading me to the cemetery gate and through and out, and shutting it between us. "Me too." He pulled the latchjaw over the latch. "God be with you," he said to shoo me.

I marched away, around the high cemetery fence the church put up between the ones who have reached God and the ones who are still waiting. I was thinking of that song about the three kings, but I drew a blank on the words, so I had to make them up. I sang, "Washington. Lincoln. Hamilton Hamilton. Hamilton Hamilton Hamilton Hamilton." My marching music. Eusebio wanted to count his money alone, I could guess that much.

I went out of my way to find the Bishop's small brick home. Behind it was a greenhouse. Ringing his property were young poplars and ringing his home were clumps of giant, elderly pricklypear cactus. Their wine-red fruit was starlit. He had a brass doorknocker cross on his front door, a small door window above the cross. "Pray for me," I said to the No-One-in-Particular who is the Holy Ghost. "Gimme this day my daily bread and I'll leave Eusebio, my old friend, alone, the sitting duck with about a hundred and seventy bucks, who wouldn't have to even know it was me that took it, would he?"

I thought about the Bishop's rooms where two pictures of a Mexican revolutionary, Lieutenant Manuel Hernández Galván, hung on the walls near Saint Joan and Teresa of Ávila. Saint Bridget. Saint Monica. Above them all, Our Lady of Guadalupe. Each block I walked farther from the Bishop's house, I imagined myself that much more comfortable in every room of it. As I put my hands in my coat pockets, and deeper, and imagined them in the scalding, soapy water filling the

Bishop's kitchen sink, I pretended I was with him: I said, "You have so many knives."

In my dream, he hummed. He said, "Yes, my friend. Yes, but I have no bread knives. No bread knives, and I eat so much more bread and butter than meat." He was using a steak knife to make thin slices of egg. He peppered each slice and held it up like the Holy Sacrament and ate it with amazed pleasure. He was so happy!

I washed the hot knife edges with my fingertips. It would be satisfying to buy my friend the Bishop his own butter knives. I would buy him two at Eastertime. Maybe I would buy him an egg slicer, one of those too, so he could have perfect golden sections.

"Come now, Red. Eat."

"When I'm finished washing everything clean," I said. He was my buddy, my best friend since childhood, though you can see we lived in different parts of God's earthly kingdom. Whenever I was out of work, he hired me as caretaker of Christ Is King. Above everyone's objections, he hired and rehired me. "I am the Bishop," he answered the skeptics. "I am authorized."

I turned around then in my walk, and cut back through the cemetery, our cemetery, our rings of stones radiating outward from the Virgen de Guadalupe, who stands at the center. Under her feet is the inscription *Reina de México y Emperatriz de América*. It is the Christ Is King cemetery but the Mother of God is caretaker for all the souls there. So many are the childhood friends of Eusebio and the Bishop and me. Oidora Zorita, Pete Bustamante, Albert Ulloa, Purísima Beaumont, Gus Hillers, Laurencia Guerra, the communion of saints.

I tiptoed to a hidden place behind a mulberry tree where I could spy on Eusebio standing in the middle of those frozen fencepost holes. He had the money still bunched up in his wool trouser pockets, four pockets, deep enough. His head bowed to his chest. He kneeled, buried all the money in one hole, barely covering it. He stood, kicked in the edges. His hands held the front collar of his coat, muddy fists pressed together under his chin.

I thought, What're you waiting for, Eusebio? I thought this too: What're you waiting for, Red? I looked around. I won't say there wasn't a soul there in the cemetery because the souls were everywhere, no question about it. Like anyone alone too many years, I have sought their company.

He looked down at the other holes or into them, at the frozen soup of mud, or what, or what, Eusebio? The little bowls of darkness.

He dove deep into one of them with his eyes and hands and whole curved body. You could see him dive without really moving. Okay, I thought, I won't. You keep your money, Eusebio. There would be more money at the end of Advent than at the beginning. I could wait.

As if he were answering me, Eusebio crossed himself, pressing his thumb and first two fingers, really pressing them, into his forehead, chest, and left and right shoulder. In a kind of very quiet, clear Spanglish he began to pray. I listened to just the first part because by then I'd made up my mind to rob him of nothing, not his money or his secrets, until I could have a greater quantity of both. I heard only this much: "I am begging you."

The next night Eusebio's lot again had twelve ragged Mexican eversomethings leaning out of their fencepost holes like they had bad attitudes or very pure motives. I was beginning to think the trees came from a golf course or a city park, and I said that to Eusebio who said, "From Mexico. My cousin, he brings them."

I asked, "He lives in Mexico?"

"*Comes here* from Mexico."

"When?" I asked. "When does he come?" Eusebio wouldn't say more, and I asked, "What's he charge you?"

"Nada." Eusebio wanted to convince me he wasn't lying. He put his well-groomed face into the soft light around the flashlight's bright beam. "Nada."

"Do you pay him anything?" I asked.

He shook his head no, no, no, enough nos to be lies or sure truths.

I put my own face into that halo of light to be closer. "Nothing. You pay nothing?"

"Nada."

"It's a sin. To come so far—for nothing."

He put his fingers on the dial to adjust his hearing aid. Why would he do that except to hear me better?

He brought two customers inside the cemetery to visit his trees. When he closed the gate behind them, the husband looked at me looking at them. Sometimes people see me reaching for their company, overeager, putting myself too close, like Recita does. They see the clock behind my face questioning them about how long it will be, long until they buy the tree, take it into the shelter of their home. And where it will stand, that must be decided. And where are the ornaments that must be dug out of the back of the closet. Undressing, probably ashamed of his middle-age middle, the husband asks, "Couldn't we buy bubble lights, red bubble lights, dear?" How long until he asks, "Really, dear, really, please, why not?" Her asleep and smiling, smiling and disappearing from their home, their unlighted tree, church, cemetery, the watcher at the gates, to a place out of his arms. "Why not," he says, "why not one string of those candy-cane bubble lights?" She says, "Okay." Or she says, "Shut up."

Water and wine. I pour out a version of people's lives, and, I confess, I spill some of my own life into the cup.

"Dear?" the man said. On cue, she fished money from her purse. Eusebio held the gate open for the man who had the tree hoisted onto his right shoulder. His wife's hand clamped onto his left shoulder, guiding him. Eusebio said, "God be with you," stuffing the money in his left back trouser pocket. I knew his banking method, how he put the first bunch of money in his left back pocket, then filled the right back pocket, the right front, then the left front—that was his banking ceremony.

The Bishop always said, after the final blessing, he said, "The Mass is never ended. Do not forget." In the Latin Masses he would have said, "*Ite, missa est,*" which means, "That's it." We Catholics think we know about respecting what was, what is, and what could be. When we make the sign of the cross, we promise to live in the Name of the Father and of the Son and of the Holy Spirit. So much innocence and arrogance, all at once.

Who would guess that I receive communion at Mass? Me? My soul is a dark-tinted beer bottle, but it holds the Spirit the same as crystal.

"Eusebio," I said when both of us were sitting together again in front of his sign, "you ever go to Mass anymore?"

He didn't answer. Later in Advent, I asked again.

He said an uncertain no.

"You're a liar, Eusebio." I could see him, see right into him, because the moon behind him was almost a whole silver coin. Bright snowclouds moved in the sky, reaching for the moon and missing.

He said it was a long story. He would not tell me. He was close enough that the sapsmell of him burned my nose. Pine needles shone in his white hair. He asked, "Why should I tell?"

He wanted to tell, he wanted to. I thought, How long will it be, Eusebio? I said, "It's Advent. In a few days it will be Christmas. You should share."

"Oh," he said. "You mean the money."

"You should share."

"It is not mine," he said. "If it was mine I would give you all of it."

That night he sold his last tree to Recita, whose hands closed over the money she had put in his hand. She said she knew why he was there selling Christmas trees. "Do you think I don't?" she asked.

Eusebio said he didn't know, he was sorry. He tried to extract his hand from her and her money.

She pulled him closer—I think she wanted a closer look at his ears' plus and minus signs—and asked, "Are you forgiven now, Eusebio?" She gave him his hands back, the money, four Washingtons, two Lincolns, falling to his feet. "I was your stepsister's friend."

Eusebio said, "Yes." He said it to her Christmas tree. He lifted the tree into his arms. "I remember." How he held the tree, I'll never forget, his arms pinning all its arms down. Down, I mean, and trees' arms reach up, don't they?

Recita asked, "How old was her baby?"

"I remember," he said. "An infant."

The rest she said to me though she meant it for Eusebio. "In 1942, his stepsister and her husband, they brought the infant here from Mexico, they needed help. They thought they would find help here, here with you, Eusebio, in this country because, after all . . ."

Eusebio rushed toward her car with the tree in his arms.

"Who could offer more? You own fifty-six rooms!"

She stood close to me, too close, I said to myself. At a distance from us, his body rocking, bent over, Eusebio dove from terrible heights without ever moving.

Recita's words now were meant for me, for me and all the solitary souls in the cemetery to whom she had not given her witness. "God knows how many keys to how many rooms you had, Eusebio!"

Eusebio leaned the tree against her closed car trunk and stayed looking into the branches.

"The sickness was like this," she said, closing one fist and opening it in an instant, her fingers trembling there between us. "Baby, mother, father. Gone."

She asked, "You are Eusebio's friend?"

"Eusebio?" I swallowed his name like a cup of dust. "Me?"

"You are his friend," she said.

How do *I* know, old woman? That is what I might have said, but she left me and went to her car. All the words she spoke to Eusebio there were sharpened sticks: "Do you not feel ashamed? Do you forget? Do you—?" Eusebio wept and mumbled, "Yes. Yes. Yes." She straightened him up with an embrace, imprisoning and tough, and as tender as I've ever seen woman give man. Moonlight made her simple straw-gold dress shine like a polished chalice. For twenty-five years I have loved her. Before Cecilia died I had already fallen in love with Recita. Which was the greater sin: to love Recita, or to love two women?

Without saying goodnight, I marched away. Her litany and his sorrowful vows were my marching music. "Do you? Do you? Do you?" "Yes. Yes."

At the Bishop's house, I could not help myself. I thought about the money. Washington Lincoln Hamilton Hamilton.

I thought about Cecilia. La Memoria. At Christmas I would set a place for her at my kitchen table in order to invite the memory of her back. La Memoria would sit with me. La Memoria and I would bring another pillow from the closet. We would be together all night, but only for the one night.

I marched and imagined. I found myself at the mulberry tree again, watching Eusebio pray at the fencepost holes, the muddy votive bowls of moonlight. And this time I listened carefully to every word he meant only for God to hear. The praying lasted almost one hour. My freezing fingers held on tight to the tree, like they were holding the top rungs of a tall, swaying ladder. My nose leaked, but blowing, even wiping, might make noise. I kneeled to relax my neck and relieve my back.

After he was gone, I rescued the Christmas tree Recita had left behind. I carried it through the gate and tried to help it stand in a hole shallower than the others.

I had to dig a little.

In the new year, at the confessional, I told the Bishop all of this. He listened to everything.

"I like the part about me," he said. "It is a lucky thing to be in a story, and I'm thankful, Red."

Through the caning between us, I couldn't see him the way I wanted to. Very quietly—he was excited as he whispered it—he said, "God's plots are weird, no?"

Weird? Yes, I thought, very weird.

"Do you know," the Bishop said, "that Eusebio was robbed on Christmas Eve? All his money was dug up from where he buried it!"

"No!" I said, sinning right there in the confessional.

"Do you know," he said, "Eusebio was selling the trees to raise money for the new St. Albert the Great church?"

He explained how the priests on their bicycles delivered the trees to Eusebio. "Red! You should have seen," he said. "A tree on the handlebars and one on the rack. They wrecked all the time! The poor trees!"

"When?" I demanded. "When'd they do it?"

"Before their morning prayers," he said. "In the dark."

He was laughing, the picture of it amused him so much. I wanted to beg him not to, not to laugh.

He then told how selling the trees was Eusebio's penance for a terrible sin. He explained the deaths of the infant, the parents. The church had taken them in, and Recita Holguín had nursed them, dear Recita. It was too late for them anyway, Eusebio could not have saved them. He must have thought he recognized contagion in their suffering. It must be what we all think. But he might have given them what he could: hope, trust. He might have surprised them. With love.

The Bishop said, "He cannot forgive himself. He wants more penance. I tell him it doesn't matter. Why should it?" His face came very close to the caning between us. "Penance," he said, "is not for God. It is for the sinner who has not forgiven himself. Do you know this, Red?"

My kneeler in the confessional had springs in it. For a moment, I must have become lighter or heavier because they squeaked beneath me. I tried to stand up.

"Do you?" he asked.

I kneeled again, but I didn't answer him. What saint to pray to? Patron saint of what? I closed my eyes, pressed my palms together. *Make a temple with your hands* was what I had been taught.

The heart is many hands, one lifting up another like the petals of a flower." My mother told me this. My mother knew. She also knew the healing methods and prayers, and she would tell them as soon as you asked, no matter who you were or why you asked. "They fell into my apron," she said. "I swept them from the tables where I heard them. Crumbs!"

This was true, because she waited tables for many years at Gamboa's Restaurant, a place all the saints and satans of Las Almas passed through for generations. They came to Gamboa's, and many, but especially the women, asked if my mother would wait on them. "The priestess of Gamboa's," my father called her, who believed in her holy orders above all others. He had the faith, but he could not hold it, my father. His love for the One True Church of Stained Glass, Gold, and Imported Marble sickened and confused him, and he confessed this in tears to me many times, even when I was small, how the Church of the High Walls and Steep Steps and Closed Doors made him ashamed. That he and my mother had baptized and initiated me into the Church of the Poisoned Cup and Poisoned Bread made him suffer self-horrors he could not keep secret. After my First Confession, months passed before he returned to the church; and after my First Holy Communion and after my Confirmation, the same happened. Through Advent, Christmas, Ordinary Time, Lent, Easter.

There are Catholics and fallen Catholics. My father was a falling Catholic. He would return to the Church in shame, sooner or later he always would. There he would make his confession in order to heal his covenant with the Faith, receive the Blessed Sacrament, be reconciled again to the ancient sacrificial rituals. His new state of grace never held. And God, whose sense of humor is everlasting, had given my mother charge of ministering to this one wandering lamb and Gamboa's flock as well.

She would seat them, serve water and coffee, collect their menus, and ask, "You will eat?" When she served the food, she asked, "You have enough?" She stood back then, drawing you and everyone at your table into her eyes, which seemed to widen at the wonder she read in you. Her lips moved. Her hands fluttered from her apron pockets, her palms turned out, her fingers curved up, and like swifts writing their souls in the air, her hands fluttered back. She did not make a show of blessing you and your food in this way. Besides, the food was Maggie Gamboa's, and it was already blessed, God knows.

For most people, this was enough: her blessing and Maggie's enchiladas or tamales. But sometimes a person asked my mother if she would help with a personal problem.

This was all whispered, the same way it is in the church. You understand—can you see?—my mother's altars over which she presided, setting the table, serving the food, refilling the cups and glasses, piling plates and platters atop each other. The soothing clicking of the china, the rattling of the silverware. You feel you can tell her anything. She rubs your table with her rag—you tell her that your son has threatened your ex-husband with a knife, that your mother-in-law will not forgive you for what she learned about that man in Vado. My mother's rag, a child's old undershirt, rubs at your table—you tell her a herd of ghost goats has come each night since Easter, all the innocents you and your husband ever killed for fiestas. Your secret is shared, already you begin to feel absolved. The rag makes the blue ceramic tiles on the table turn darker and then bright. "If I tell you, you will pray this?" my mother asks.

Yes, you say. I will. Yes.

"Only what I tell you—no more—not any different?"

Yes, Mrs. Greet. In truth, I will.

PORTRAIT OF PANCHO VILLA'S LIEUTENANT, MANUEL HERNÁNDEZ GALVÁN, SHOOTING A PESO AT FIFTY PACES

Lieutenant Manuel Hernández Galván tapped my shoulder and drew a bead on me with his head. "Red," he said, "is this fair?"

"No," I said, pleased with myself.

Because she had asked me, I was dancing with his date, Carmelita Rubio, old as a three-finger baseball glove. And beautiful as such a glove is. This was the New Year's Fiesta at Christ Is King church. The Feast of the Epiphany in Las Almas, New Mexico. 1944. Fifty years ago. These are facts. You must take my word.

Near us, my wife Cecilia danced with Father Francisco Velasco. People will say a priest should not dance, and should not dance good if he dances at all. Ignorant people with no antidote for all the Virtue poisoning them say that to dance is dangerous for a priest, and to dance good is to break the celibacy vow. Cecilia danced good with him, and they swayed, they hovered. Like branches in wind, their arms swept each other's arms. They danced too good, I admit this. But I loved Frank Velasco, loved Cecilia, and the two kinds of love I felt were blue and red flame and part of the same fire.

My right hand was opened, and pressed against Carmelita

Rubio's hunched back. She cradled my neck with one hand and rested her other bare arm upon my own. She did not look at me, did not speak. The coldness of her flesh excited me.

The fiddle made the good sound of a bad door hinge in the music. That was Liston Potter, the fiddler, who was Cecilia's uncle. When Cecilia was a child, he made kites for her and her friends, Liz Why, Margaret Loving Middleton, Agnes Perea, Libby Tolentino, and the three sisters Úbeda.

This was our tenth wedding anniversary. Cecilia and I married on January 2, 1934, when we were twenty-five years old. There was much I knew about her. And much I did not.

I said to Father Velasco, "You are humming." He was not humming to the music, he was only humming. He was humming, and hovering, and swaying with my wife in his arms.

He did not hear me. Cecilia heard, and repeated it to him over the screechy singing of the blind and musically disabled singer for the band, Los Zopilotes.

Father Velasco pivoted so that Cecilia's back was to me, and he said, "I apologize," which meant for everything. For everything, he wished to have my absolution.

"Look!" said Carmelita. "Father Velasco. The man dances!"

"He sure does," I said.

My mother waved. She and Maggie Gamboa served food at the tables around us in the Christ Is King parish hall. Sadness darkened my mother's dark face. "Mexican-cinnamon" was how my father described her beautiful skin. My father had died that same year, 1944. He had laid down in the shade of a stone wall he was building for the three sisters Úbeda. Their payment paid for his funeral. I loved him, my father. I missed him. The part of his wall that I completed is the only part of the wall that now, fifty years later, needs repair.

Carmelita's cool arm moved over mine. The soft inside of

her arm. This was no accident. I noticed, yes, and wouldn't you? *Old,* I said to myself, *widow.* Only an accident that we touched this way. An accident.

Her fingers on my neck crept into the hair behind my ear. Two fingers trembled over the crescent of smoothness there. The back of her cold thumb brushed the lobe, which filled with blood. What music was playing? I could not hear it through that clanging ear. Did I move my feet? My feet had stopped. Of themselves they had stopped.

I gave myself more medicine against this. *Decaying,* I said. *Petrified.*

"Doña Carmelita. What do you—mean?" I asked.

Somehow her satin dancing slippers held me still.

"You," I said, "you. You. You are standing on my feet. Are you standing on my feet?" I could not look down. She offered her fragrant white hair to the tender purse of flesh under my chin. I was forty years younger than her. I was barely thirty-five years old. If she had spoken, could she have been more obscene in her bravery with my body?

"Mr. Greet," said Antonio Velasco. "I wish you a happy anniversary." He was Father Velasco's father. And leading him over the dance floor was Mrs. V.

"Thank you," I said.

"*Gracias,*" Cecilia said, one hand on Father Velasco's shoulder, one closed hand in the center of his back, closed and maybe clasping his white priest's shirt. I had white shirts like that one. I had eight of them. Stolen. I am ashamed to tell about them.

Carmelita's bright black *chaleco,* her vest, swung open, and on the inside I saw the pattern I had not noticed on the outside: small vermilion snakes chasing large green ones. Her nose, the icy tip, rubbed against the plum in my throat. Have you touched this hard fruit with your own fingers? And can you ever know its ripeness as you can through another's touch?

"Again," she whispered.

"Again?" I asked. "What do you mean?"

I could move my feet once more. My arms fell to my sides. She had said this "again" into my throat, but she had not said it to me.

Lieutenant Galván answered her, "All the night would please me, Carmelita."

I said, "Have mercy." I wanted to say something more clever. I felt the need of cleverness to hide my lust.

He said, "Doña Carmelita is too hot for you, Red."

No cleverness would come. None. Slowly, through the broken fences around my thoughts, I found words I once saw on a gravestone: "One must do battle to prepare for war." I said this to the lieutenant: "One must do battle to prepare for war." And I said, "She was helping me hold back the other women."

He danced away with her, his boots tapping the floor between her black slippers. When Lieutenant Galván captured her, this dove, this soothing, soaring shadow, delicate lace of frost, sleeping buried tulip, this silver bowl of unmelting snow—when he spread his hand over her hunched back, I was pronouncing her beauty inside me. How can I help pronouncing it now? The benedictions of an old man who thirsts.

Recita Holguín danced with me then. Too close. Her long hair streamed down her back. I wished to dance with my wife Cecilia, but there was the distraction of Liston and the careening, blind, musically ungifted singer and Los Zopilotes, and my throat burned wonderfully, and Recita's hair was black, coppery red, and silver, and since she was our friend, if she asked me to dance I had the Obligation, did I not?

The next morning at Doña Carmelita's ranch Father Velasco and I met with Lieutenant Galván, and Galván's ten-year-old son Cleophas, and the famous photographer, who were Doña Carmelita's guests.

Father Velasco had arranged the photographer's visit. He was a priest and not a bishop yet. The photographer, who had photographed Lieutenant Galván in Mexico twenty years before, in 1924 (a famous picture), wanted to take the same kind of photograph again. A photograph of Lieutenant Galván shooting a peso at fifty paces.

The photographer would not cross the border into Mexico this time. It was wartime. The border guards annoyed him, he said. He needed Lieutenant Galván to cross instead. Father Velasco, who said he owed the photographer a favor, hosted the reunion between the two men. Famous men. He recruited me as their guide around Las Almas. My soul knows the reason *I* said yes. I said yes because I loved him, Father Velasco. He had been my closest friend since grade school. I would commit any sin in his service. This was my reason. (But I ask you: What favors does a priest owe to anyone except to God and other priests?)

So. We met Lieutenant Galván at the ranch gate. It had an iron arch fifteen, sixteen feet high, and on the arch: *Aquí la puerta es corazón siempre abierta.*

He said, "Go ahead."

I said, "I like the words." How is iron made into words?

A dirt path led through Doña Carmelita's small pecan orchard. In his tan long-sleeve shirt and khaki pants, with his young son at his side, Lieutenant Galván, over eighty years old at that time, looked like he commanded the uneven ranks of her trees.

Doña Carmelita met us at her door, fitting her hand inside the lieutenant's hand when she greeted him. She wore a tan blouse, a colorful jacket and skirt, a white wool stocking cap over her white hair, one snowfall upon another, one blessing blessed, and her wrinkled skin darkest bronze. Hunched the way she was hunched, she was the noblest piñon, the kind that grows from broken boulders in our mountains.

I said, "I like your words. On your gate."

"Me too," said Father Velasco.

She said nothing. Who knows if she heard us? How is iron made into words? It must be heated. It must be cooled.

She and the boy wanted to come along with us. The photographer, a termite in eyeglasses, chewed with his eyes, chewing at the boy Cleophas and her and at her small patio she walked us to. He explained that she and the boy would break the concentration of Lieutenant Galván, and his own, too, if they came. "Intense concentration in marksmanship, my dear. And greater in the art of photography. You cannot conceive of the difficulties," he said.

She said, "You *will* take Red Greet?"

The photographer had no wish to be polite. "Red is a man," he said.

"Yes," I said.

Father Velasco and Lieutenant Galván said nothing. Nothing, and yet they both looked at her closely, which caused me to look. On her face and neck, she had white down, white against her darkest bronze skin. White at the corners of her lips.

I had been close enough once before to see this down on her. In Columbus, New Mexico, I had been at the funeral of Carmelita's husband, Jimmy Rubio, who had been a bad man—and my father's friend. And I saw this frost around her mouth and on her throat when she reached into the open coffin. Everyone saw. She reached in to pull Jimmy Rubio's pockets, all four, inside out. "Where is it?" she asked Jimmy, who was not likely to answer. "Where is it?"

Strange grief. God alone understands. And what about the "it" she looked for? Did she think Jimmy had asked someone to put it in the pockets of his burial clothes? Was it something he had taken from her?

We left her behind. We walked into the desert north of

her home. Murmuring turtledoves fell silent and flung themselves from the creosote and mesquite. Their wings made blessings in the air, which was full of good burning desert incenses. We—the photographer and Lieutenant Galván, Father Velasco and I—we talked about the *it*. I had told them Jimmy Rubio's funeral story because we had four things that reminded me. Father Velasco had God's grace, which creates time. I had the pesos—the money—which measures time. The photographer had the camera, which seizes time. And Lieutenant Galván, he had the gun, which erases time. How could I not remember? One of his hands held the carved ivory grip of the Colt .45, and one hand anchored the other hand. True aim. Seven and one half inches of polished barrel, silver-plated.

Lieutenant Galván walked in short steps. He wore big, sharp Mexican spurs that made a warning jingle horses and horsemen could understand. But I think his legs were not strong. The night before, his legs had run far on the dance floor. The photographer and Father Velasco and I slowed down to be respectful.

"Your boots," I said to the lieutenant, "are not good."

"You see right," he said. "They shame me."

"Unfortunate," said Father Velasco.

The photographer said, "They *are wonderful.*" I knew that already he had made a mental picture: noble, ancient boots. He gilded them with Mexican dust and the blood of Villistas and Zapatistas. Imagining a little further, he might picture them being taken from a dead man. We walked toward a small jacal and a cluster of tamarisk, and, above them, a dinosaur fig tree that bowed over them like a hand in its hundredth year of slowly closing. An old tree is more patient than anything.

We were quiet, but inside us we were unrestful. I remembered Cecilia's hand, her right hand clutching the white cloth of Father Velasco's shirt. I remembered Recita Holguín leading me over the dance floor. And Elizabeth Velasco leading Antonio Velasco. And Liz and Margaret and Libby taking turns dancing with each other, taking turns leading.

I told my theory about the *it* that Carmelita Rubio had looked for in Jimmy's pocket. "The *it* was stolen by Jimmy Rubio," I said. "Carmelita's mother's golden pin, something worth fortunes. A key to a lockbox!"

"Or something sacred—holy," said Father Velasco.

The photographer said, "I feel it would have been something sentimentally invaluable. Perhaps a belt or comb." He asked Lieutenant Galván, "What do you think?"

Lieutenant Galván said, "She was a *soldadera*."

Soldadera. The photographer was probably already engraving the word upon his dull brain.

"A s*oldadera?*" asked Father Velasco. He wore the same white shirt he had worn at the fiesta. I wore a white shirt too, but fresh.

"She was a *soldadera*," said the lieutenant. "A soldier in the revolution."

"She told you this?" I asked.

"No," he said. "I know."

"Splendid!" said the photographer, who I could not like, I tell you.

The lieutenant said, "I met her once back then. I had known her—" Whatever he wanted to tell, he withheld. Instead, he said, "She was famous."

At first, I doubted him. "Famous?" I asked.

"As a saint is," he said.

When he said this, I believed. With no cause, I suddenly did not doubt at all this fact about Señora Rubio. (I am Catholic. I disbelieve. I believe. I disbelieve. Amen.)

Father Velasco believed too, but this was his nature and not mine. He said, "*Soldadera!* Of course!"

I wanted Lieutenant Galván to tell us more, but he stepped under the shadows of the fig tree. He placed his gun on the roof of the jacal, which was no more than a falling-down doghouse of juniper branches.

"I met her on a train," Lieutenant Galván said. "She commanded this train. She had lieutenants. Many. And armed troops of women." He asked me, "You have the peso?"

I had a pocketful of them that I punched so they jangled like Lieutenant Galván's spurs.

The photographer looked at me. He imagined nothing at all on my face or in my head. I felt his eyes chewing me, and I looked at my shoes. They were nothing special. I looked at Father Velasco's shoes. Newly resoled—the loot of the cobbler Amezquita who gave the priests in our town the shoes unclaimed by his customers.

"It would be best," the photographer said, "if we would rehearse." He explained to me that they had rehearsed, after all, even in 1924 when he took the first famous picture of Lieutenant Galván, sixty years old then. He told me they had no third or fourth persons with them in Mexico. But it was "splendid" to have us along, and since we were along, we were to walk fifty paces away. The photographer would stay near Lieutenant Galván.

The lieutenant pointed. "Pace fifty south," he said. "How high you can throw—throw that high."

Father Velasco walked the fifty paces with me. I had wondered whether he would stay with them or with me.

The photographer planted his wooden tripod low on the ground and aimed the camera up at the lieutenant to make him look big as a war monument. This was how he took the picture in 1924 also. I know this method: with only the essence of a truth, you make perfume.

When I tossed the first peso it went high and away. Lieutenant Galván swung his arm and fist up. Calm. Smooth.

In one motion of his index finger he squeezed an imaginary trigger. And missed. By a mile, he missed.

I knew I could not find that peso. I didn't look.

The next peso I threw up straighter but not high. Lieutenant Galván pretending, shooting again with his empty hand, missed it. How far? Far. If the gun had been in his hand, the picture would be a portrait of Pancho Villa's lieutenant, Manuel Hernández Galván, shooting Red Greet in the face at fifty paces.

I caught the peso. I held it up, proud because I had caught it. In a single action, Lieutenant Galván pretended to shoot at the shining target in my fingers. Missed by a mile. We both laughed. He pretended to shoot Father Velasco, who thumped his chest and said, "Got me."

The photographer crouched down, aimed his camera up to make Lieutenant Galván big as he might look in history books.

The lieutenant picked up the gun now, turned it in his right hand, his eyes traveling along the barrel as along a train track. He held the Colt out for the camera to see, but he was not thinking about the gun. He said, "You know this *it*. This is what I believe: *it* was a picture of Doña Carmelita. Jimmy Rubio wanted a picture of his wife to keep with him in hell."

"My God!" said the face behind the camera. The beauty of a photograph is its silence. A photographer should know this. But the photographer said, "That is *quite good*."

Lieutenant Galván brushed the silver barrel across his thick silver mustache. He was smelling the steel. "Jimmy had a photograph of her when she was young," he said. "Doña Carmelita was naked in this photograph. Naked and pregnant."

"My God!" said the termite voice of the camera.

"Jesus Mary Joseph," said Father Velasco, because God's name had now been taken in vain twice.

Lieutenant Galván pointed the gun at the termite photographer and motioned a certain way with his shoulders to ask me if he should.

"Go ahead," I said. I meant: Put us out of our misery. Shoot him.

His tiny head behind the camera, the photographer grunted the word, "Naked."

"She was maybe not all naked," said Lieutenant Galván. "She was showing off her gun and her ammunition belts. Naked except for her gun and ammunition belts. This was the photograph Jimmy stole from her to take with him."

Whether she was naked or armed, whether she was naked *and* armed, where Jimmy was going everyone would want to see. They would get to look, and she did not want this. The history of her body. The history of her soul. Would you want Jimmy Rubio to have this?

The photographer's head, a puppet head, a finger inside it where the brain should be, popped out from behind the camera. "Everything, all the light, and this breeze, is marvelous," said the photographer. "We must go on." He motioned to us where we should stand. First, he pretended to take a picture of Lieutenant Galván shooting the gun at nothing. This was the rehearsal. The photographer pretended he was shooting pictures. The lieutenant was shooting real bullets, reloading.

"Shoot," he said to Lieutenant Galván. "Again. Again."

The photographer made him step out of the shadows and bring the Colt near his face. He asked him to shoot the gun in the single action a Model P is made to shoot. Next, he asked the lieutenant to fan the hammer as if killing six.

Father Velasco stood right next to me through all this, all of this. Recita Holguín had danced at least as close to me as Father Velasco had with Cecilia. Carmelita Rubio and I had danced with her cool arms moving over my arms.

The lieutenant's left profile was better than his right

because his left eye squinted half-closed when he aimed. He shot many bullets. He obliged the photographer. Reloaded.

Afterward, the photographer said, "There is so much smoke, isn't there?" Disappointed. The cordite smelled no different from the air of the desert, no different really.

When the rehearsing was over, it was time to take the real photographs.

I have a donkey's heart. I was afraid. Father Velasco calmed me. "Fountain of Heaven. Mother of God. Ark of Peace," he said. A blessing.

Lieutenant Galván could see I was afraid, and he said, "High as you can throw."

The photographer said, "Say 'NOW' before you toss it up there."

Father Velasco stood closer. The coin grew cold in my fingers. Colder and colder. Smaller and smaller.

"NOW!" I said.

The picture happened fast.

The photographer took one shot at the instant the lieutenant took one shot.

Missed by a mile.

We all walked to where we thought the peso fell. We walked slow, I think, to not have to look at one another. We knew the peso was unwounded, whole.

"Over here," said Lieutenant Galván.

He dropped his own peso, shiny, fresh from his shirt pocket, onto a patch of sand white as paper. He stood with the toes of his boots almost on the peso's edges. Unblinking, he aimed and shot a hole through it.

What were we supposed to say? The priest did not know. The famous photographer did not know. The famous lieutenant did not. Only I, unfamous Red Greet, had ever found himself in such a lion's den of need. I said, "Your boots! You could have ruined them!"

Father Velasco picked up the coin. He handed it to me. I looked through the hole at Father Velasco, at the photographer, at Manuel Hernández Galván. I looked so close through the coin my eye felt the heat of the metal. With my mind I took the picture of the truth, nothing like the famous picture.

I said, "Perfect!"

"Good shooting!" said the photographer.

"Amazing," said Father Velasco.

"It was," said Lieutenant Galván. Not a lie.

On the walk back, Lieutenant Galván said, "She broke my concentration."

We could not disagree. We had spoken of Doña Carmelita when we should not have.

To shoot, Lieutenant Galván had taken off his sombrero. He put it on again, not using the chin strap, which dangled at the back of his neck. He held the gun in front of him, below his waist. With one hand Lieutenant Galván held the carved ivory grip of the gun, and with one hand he held the other hand. Just as before. Such weakness, so complete, I have seen only in men. We passed the fig tree and her odd children, the tamarisks.

"She was a killer," the lieutenant said. "A killer." He walked in short steps. We could not walk as slow. We heard him behind us say, "The *soldadera* song. All about her."

Even I, Red the donkey, knew the anthem of the heroic *soldaderas* was "Adelita." I would not correct him, a witness to the revolution. But the books say the song was "Adelita," not Carmelita.

"She was a killer." Lieutenant Galván said this again, "She was a killer." He could not keep up with us, and we walked ahead until we could hear nothing more that he might say.

"A sinner," said Father Velasco. Maybe he meant Carmelita Rubio. Maybe, Lieutenant Galván.

On her patio, she had prepared tea for us. The boy poured it into china cups. The saucers were hand-painted with tiny blue crocuses and rose leaves and delicate thorns.

"I have made it weak," she said, "but I have sugar. And fresh lemon."

She served us warm, moist *bizcochitos*. Dark. Coated in powdered sugar. She had made them that afternoon.

It would have been improper for her to ask us anything. She knew this and she waited. The boy, a severe look in his eyes, a wild grin on his mouth, sat next to her.

The lieutenant took out the peso to show them. He and the photographer told the story. Slowly, they told the story, feeling their way along the path of it. In the newspapers and magazines their way was how the story was told. In the photographer's books, their words were like carved ivory. Father Velasco said nothing. I said nothing.

Before they found their way to the story's end, she rested her hands on the boy's shoulders, looked down at the gun on the violet tablecloth covering the patio table.

The way they told what they told is as you see it in the famous picture, more famous now than the first picture.

Invincible old man in bright sunlight.

No smoke.

Eyes fixed on a miracle.

The photographer said, in the newspapers and the magazines, he said *he* tossed the coin himself. He tossed the coin, he pressed the trigger of his camera, and he shot his one picture— a shot as true as the one shot of Manuel Hernández Galván, Pancho Villa's lieutenant.

Red Greet was not there, you see? And Father Francisco Velasco. Not there. Erased.

And Señora Carmelita Rubio? And Cleophas Galván?

Never mentioned. No one mentions them. The gun, a

gift from the lieutenant, she took into the grave with her, so people say. I was there the next year, in '45, at her funeral. I touched the white angeldown on her nose and chin and at the corners of her cold lips. Yes, I touched it. Death gives permission.

She had given the peso to Cleophas Galván.

"Red!" said my confessor. Bishop Francisco Velasco knew all along it was me across from him in the confessional. Yes. Now, so many years later, he was a bishop. And yet he heard confessions once a month. He could not abstain from hearing stories. He liked especially the stories that he was in.

"Red!" he said, amazed and thrilled. "History is a great sin! But it is not *your* sin!"

"Are you sure?" I asked.

"I was there," he said. "I was there!"

In that little room with all the carpeting and curtains, his laughing was much like weeping. I worried that Recita Holguín or Mr. Holy-in-the-Front-Pew might have been waiting in the line for confession.

He put his head close to the caning between us. "I cannot absolve this."

"So?"

"So. I cannot absolve a sin that is not your sin."

"Nothing?"

He sounded like he was picking his teeth. He was picking his teeth or taking his chewing gum out. Where to put it? He said, "God's ways!"

He began his own confession, confessing to himself. "Bless me, Father, for I have sinned," he said. "I have become Red Greet's confessor. I am Red Greet's friend. I never believed Red Greet would come to confession sinless. Hell would freeze first! And for these things I ask forgiveness."

I should not tell this, but he was laughing.

He absolved himself, more absolution than the usual. He gave himself many penances, more than the usual. He resolved to sin no more.

He asked me, "You like potatoes?" At first, I thought he was still talking to himself, since he had cooked potatoes for me many times. "I slice them thick," he said, "put lard in an iron pan, chop in chiles, onion, big wedges of yellow onion, salt, cilantro. You like potatoes like this?" Before I could answer, he said, "I know you do."

Onions and chiles and potatoes! Jonah, who was spat from the darkness, did not feel as blessed as I did.

"So?" the Bishop said.

I received no absolution. I was given no penance. I made the sign of the cross. I resolved to sin no more because that is how confession ends no matter what. I opened the door to the confessional.

"Anybody else out there?" the Bishop asked from his dark booth.

"No one," I said.

If the problem was that you were dying, if your body or soul was dying, my mother wrote her telephone number on a blank receipt ticket and pressed it in your hand. She offered the restaurant's starched white napkins for your tears and runny nose. She waited. You could do all your crying, wiping, honking your nose empty, and still she waited, standing near you.

When you finished, she said, "Don't steal Señora Gamboa's napkin, okay?" Dear Mother, dearest Ana, were you thinking of me when you said this?

One Saturday afternoon, the blazing hot fifth of July, Mrs. Gamboa's ceiling fans going the one slow speed they went, the ungreased hubs making shoveling sounds, I sat in a corner booth waiting for my mother's rag to finally stop washing the clean and unclean so I could walk home with her. Two of Gamboa's Saturday regulars, Mr. and Mrs. Aceldama, quietly talked about having a featherweight Stetson made for Mr. Alcedama. Mercedes Alcedama moved her hands over her ears and forehead, showing her husband how she thought the brim and crown should look, how she thought the brim should curve up only slightly, the crown should be a poke. And what would the hatband be? Snakeskin? Conchas? Their hands moved over each other's head, shaping wonders.

I could see their love, and I wanted to steal what part I could see. The hat, I mean. So much love in my own life then, and yet I wanted more, more of what others had, more wonders atop my own head. This hungriness of mine, since I was nine or ten years old, how do I ever tell what griefs it caused my parents?

My father had begged me to stop stealing, and then, tired of repeating himself, he silently tried to heal me of it by giving things to me: giving me a coffee can to be my own pretend well since I had stolen the Escalantes' well bucket; giving me my own plum tree since I had ripped someone else's sapling from the ground and planted it in a hidden place; giving me a dog since I had dragged away and hidden the doghouse of Flannery, the Nelsons' dog. I had planted the plum tree right next to the doghouse in the hidden place where I had made a kind of altar.

Small house. Small tree. Small well. Lovely.

My parents had so little. They worked so hard and had so little. My father gave me a hand mirror and a pair of scissors like those I had stolen from our friend Willa Hancock, who had expertly sheared herself and her daughter and our family for years. She had always refused payment and had, instead, brought us gifts of food. After she was robbed, Willa Hancock bought a new mirror and scissors and trimmed us all just as before, and, knowing everything about me, trimmed my terrier Vince, exactly according to my specifications. She asked me if Vince ever stole bones and hid them. "Dogs will do that," she said. Why did Willa love me? She did. She loved me irrationally.

My mother prayed for me. "Do you know what I pray?" she asked when my stealing angered and shamed her beyond her control. "No, you do not," she said. "You have no idea what I pray for." I admit, that would scare me into honesty for a few days at a time.

In the restaurant with my mother, I planned how I would

steal Maggie Gamboa's record book. Mrs. Velasco, a woman we knew from church, came in. I had never seen her or Mr. Velasco or their son, my friend Francisco, in the restaurant. She asked if my mother had a table free, which of course she did.

"Damn," I said, almost out loud. I was anxious to steal the record book and take it home.

Mrs. Velasco accepted water, held the glass in both hands, but did not drink. She glanced at me, mercifully glanced away. She had tears in her eyes, and I did not want to see them spill. Now, in memory, I look longer at them than I did then.

My mother gave her a menu, which Mrs. Velasco handed back. She did not have to say that she could not read the English or Spanish words on the menu, because my mother spared her this and said, "Tamales. Menudo. Like heaven." Mrs. V ordered nothing.

My mother's rag seemed to write disappearing cursive on the table. Maybe my mother was pretending she herself could write, or maybe she was only cleaning the very clean table. Mrs. V's eyes were humiliated and wanting but unwilling. The fingers inside the rag caressed the table, and the reflections of the ceiling fans made light and dark spin over the wrinkles around Mrs. V's eyes.

And how do I remember all that? I look at Mrs. V's eyes. Mrs. V. I am remembering things the way a person remembers in confession. Her eyebrows were the same thick, thorn-brown chaos as the eyebrows of my friend Francisco.

He and I were both fifteen, and I knew him from Christ Is King elementary school, where we played together, and junior high, when we recited Latin out loud in Miss Iffrig's class, and high school, when we double-dated, Arlene Úbeda and I, Cecilia and he.

Mrs. V gave my mother back the napkin. I concentrated on the "Facts about United States Currency and Coins" in Maggie Gamboa's huge record book, her ledger, the 1924

Standard Diary. I like currency and coins, the faces and plain facts of history that you can spend however you must or, if you are rich, however you please.

My mother whispered questions. Mrs. V whispered back. "Lemonade?" my mother asked. "He likes lemonade?" I heard that part. The very word made my mouth water. The ceiling fans seemed to say the word, LEMonade, LEMonade.

The two women talked a long time. My mother brought Mrs. V lemonade, and asked her to drink. Mother sat across from her and showed her how she should say certain things into the lemonade a certain way. They practiced the way, the words.

"Your husband will drink this."

"He—" Mrs. V wiped her mouth with a napkin, the napkin not moving away from her lips. One innocent kiss upon the bright cloth. Innocent and instant.

"He thirsts," Mrs. V said. She rested the cloth, a small white ghost, on the table.

THE
PASSING-BELL

Until the very day of her death, my wife Cecilia and my friend Frank did not consummate their love.

And then, before God and Recita Holguín and me, their lovemaking lasted through the Holy Viaticum, Extreme Unction, the Last Blessing and Plenary Indulgence, the Acts of Most Necessary Virtue, and the Recommendations of a Departing Soul. One whole day and night. Her body lingered before dying and her soul lingered before departing, because she did not want one sacramental intimacy with Frank. She wanted many, many intimacies of whispered prayer and passionate litany and blessing, cleansing touching and everlasting anointing, and I know this, I know this, that she wanted her final breath and final kiss to be on the crucifix he breathed upon and kissed.

Two weeks before Lent, Frank came in the morning to our home with his small suitcase, which he unpacked in our bedroom. On the clean white cloth of her bed table he placed one candlestick, a standing wooden crucifix made by the santera Sophia Gutiérrez, a spoon, a handbell, and two glasses. Into one glass, he poured holy water. Recita and I filled the other with fresh tap water as he asked us. He unwrapped one loaf of dark bread the size of a child's fist, and he examined it before he wrapped it in the oily paper again. He cooked this bread himself, a bread that smelled like grated yellow onion and scalded milk, and that tasted mildly salty: the Blessed Sacrament. He brought out wine in a pocket flask.

He opened his missal. "Peace be unto this house," he said, and he asked Recita and me to repeat the response: "And unto all who dwell therein."

We genuflected with him before the Blessed Sacrament and the flask of wine. He put his thumb and first two fingers into the glass of holy water and sprinkled Cecilia's body and her bed with it. Drops ran from her cheeks to her ears and from around her nose onto her lips, and from her bare shoulders onto her arms, and from her wrists into her half-opened hands. He sprinkled the water over her hair.

He recited, "Thou shalt sprinkle me, O Lord, with hyssop, and I shall be cleansed. Thou shalt wash me, and I shall be made whiter than snow. Have mercy upon me, O God, according to Thy great mercy."

Whenever he said, "Amen," Cecilia said, "Amen." She said, "Amen," but she was not saying, "So be it," she was saying something else.

At first, Recita and I said "Amen" with them, but that did not seem right and we stopped. We sat together at one end of the sofa in Cecilia's room. This sofa, unattractive blue, with uncomfortable cushions and a spine-torturing slatted wooden back, was motel furniture, a tenth-anniversary gift from Eusebio Gruber.

Frank asked Cecilia if she would make her confession. It was no surprise that he asked her in front of Recita and me: What sins had she committed on her deathbed that required confession? He asked her anyway.

Her mouth closed in a frown and in the next instant opened in a girlish smile. She said, "You first, Frank."

He laughed. We laughed. Not for very long.

He adjusted the pillows under her neck and head, lifting her back with his one hand on her shoulder and his other between her shoulderblades, the way he would hold her in a dance. The white sheet and thin white blanket over her were all the covering she had because the dead are meant to enter heaven humble and because the living must be humbled by death's naked embrace.

Earlier that morning I had undressed her as she had asked me to, and bathed her with a cold cloth that might soothe her, and washed her short hair in a large, shallow bowl, and brushed it forward, and made her bed the way she liked. From the chair she sat in, she saw me looking at her body, sixty-three years old, and she said, "You see me undisguised."

"Yes."

She did not ask to be covered when I laid her on the bed. "You have always seen, haven't you?" she asked.

I had always seen through her disguises, always, but I did not wish to say it. I should have said, "I love you. Of course I see." And why didn't I?

Her neck. Around her neck she wore nothing ever. She never wore a necklace, though early in our courtship I had given her necklaces. She never closed the buttons at her collar. She was overproud of her long, lovely, unwrinkled neck and the broad shoulders and expansive chest of all her people, the Chamuscados, that is. She looked wrong in light, flowery blouses, and she would not wear them even to church. She wore a man's shirt well, and I liked how she cut the collars off and sewed on bright embroidered bands. She unbuttoned the shirts to the center of her chest and, because her breasts were small and far apart, the look was bold but not openly sexy. I liked this. From birth, her heart had been injured, one chamber starved of blood and one confounded by too much. When the first heart attacks came in 1955, I begged her to have the surgery that might help. She refused. She said, "My heart is not more imperfect than yours."

She asked for her perfume, which was a concoction my mother had made for her from yellow daisies, rosemary, and boiled roses. Rubbing the scent into my hands, I perfumed her hair. On our wedding night, she had first asked this of me. Every Saturday evening after she bathed, she asked, "Red, will you come?" I patted her short wet hair, black as rain on coal, and I pushed my fingers toward her forehead, and pushed them back again, and rubbed the perfume into the soft black wisps on the back of her neck. I looked into her face, no larger than my open hand, and I wanted to touch the owl-like wrinkles under and around her eyes and her owlish brows. I should have smoothed the wrinkles on her neck and spread my hands on her chest to feel the last warmth there. And I should have said that when she died we would stand together like trees in a forest as we had for thirty-eight years because our roots and branches were that knotted together. I should have said something beautiful the way people say in books at the end. But everything beautiful that I thought was untrue. She did not want my touch. She wished to fall away from and free of me.

"Cover me," she said.

I said, "Please, Cecilia," because I wanted to look longer.

"Now," she said. I smoothed the sheets over her without touching her arms and hands.

I had helped make her ready for the Holy Viaticum. I, her husband, had helped make her ready for another man, Frank. This is not a beautiful thing to say, but it is true.

"May Almighty God have mercy on us, and forgive us our sins and bring us to life everlasting," said Frank, absolving them both of sins neither of them had confessed. He recited the Confiteor and when he quietly struck his hand against his heart and said, "Mea culpa, mea culpa, mea maxima culpa," Cecilia struck her own heart, her clenched right fist knocking the broken door. Whenever we made love she would do this to me, knock at my heart, sometimes quietly, sometimes loudly, knock there, not as if saying, "Red, I love you," but asking, "Do you love me?" or asking, "Who are you?"

Frank paged through his old missal, the 1930 edition, all its prayers in the English and Latin and the old forms. His fingers trembled. He could not find his place.

Cecilia sarcastically mumbled, "Behold—the Lamb of God."

He said, "Right! Bless you," because she had poked fun at him but also had recited the next part of the ritual for him. He lifted the Blessed Sacrament above her body and finished the prayer: "Behold Him who taketh away the sins of the world."

Three times he repeated, "Lord, I am not worthy; but only say the word, and my soul shall be healed." Cecilia moved her lips but did not speak the prayer out loud. Recita and I kneeled and said the prayer, which is a mysterious prayer, a thief's prayer. *One word, and my soul shall be healed.* Which word? Any word? Any word as long as it's the right word? "God writes us into being," Sister María Josefa used to say. "God writes us and revises us until we are the word."

Frank washed his fingers in the smallest glass of water by wetting the fingertips of each hand and rubbing the water into his palms. He dried them with the white cloth. Recita folded the rumpled cloth and put it back in its place on the table. He pinched off a piece of the bread. He ate. He poured wine into the glass of tap water. He drank. He dipped a tiny piece of the bread into the glass and fed Cecilia, who could not swallow at first and gasped and pressed her head back and shut her eyes. I started to help, but Recita shifted her hip a certain way to stop me. Frank leaned close over Cecilia and whispered some kind of command. I think he simply said, "Swallow." She smiled, gasped, swallowed. Her mouth and chin were damp with sweat.

He wiped Cecilia's mouth with his fingers. His thumbs brushed her lower lip and chin clean. His fingers and thumb lightly brushed the corners of her mouth.

The prayer that he said next is the prayer that ends the Holy Viaticum and it must be said, but I did not want it to be said. Could Frank have ended the ritual without it? Could Frank have offered another prayer? I don't know. I am not a priest.

Instead of holding his hand above her body to make the sign of the cross as he prayed the ending prayer, he rested it on edge at the center of her forehead, *on* her forehead, do you see?

He recited, "I hold Thee now, my Love and Sweetness, and will not let Thee go," which she repeated, moving her lips to breathe the words but not say them. "I gladly bid farewell to the world and all therein; and now I come with joy, my God, to Thee." He moved the edge of his hand down her nose and over her lips and chin and, slowly, her neck. His clean and blessed fingertips rested there as he read more from the missal, and she repeated, "Henceforth nothing, O good Jesus, shall part me from Thee; I am joined in Thee, O Christ; I will live in Thee and die in Thee, and if Thou wilt, abide in Thee forever. Now I live, yet not I, but Christ liveth in me. I am weary of my life; I desire to depart and to be with Christ; to me, to live is Christ, and to die is gain. I will fear no evil as I walk through the Valley of the Shadow of Death, for Thou, O Lord, art with me: as the heart panteth after the water-springs, so panteth my soul after Thee, O God; my soul hath thirsted after the strong Living God; when shall I come and appear before the Face of God? Bless me, most Loving Jesus, and let me now depart in peace, for I am Thine; and I will never let Thee go forever."

Recita also repeated the words after him. And what should I, the only quiet one in the choir, do? We all repeated after him, "O that I were joined to Thee in a blessed union forever! O that I were wholly taken up, wholly absorbed and buried in Thee!" Frank moved his hand across Cecilia's left breast to her shoulder, and across again to the center of her chest. He was taking liberties. I love him and am allowed to speak plainly about him. He was taking liberties. "O that my soul, resting sweetly in Thy arms, were altogether taken up in Thee, and blissfully enjoyed Thee, my loving God!" He moved his hand across her right breast to her shoulder, and opened his hand and held her shoulder and arm, and touched her hand, which reached for his before he took it away. He made the sign of the cross on his own body as he read, "What more have I to do with the world, my loving Jesus? Behold, there is none upon this earth that I desire beside Thee. Into thy hands, Lord Jesus, I commend my spirit. Receive me, my Love and Sweetness, that it may be well with me forever and that I may gently lay me down in peace with Thee, and take my rest. Amen."

Cecilia's dark eyes had been closed. "Amen," she said. When she opened them, they were the shadows of fire but not fire, not any longer. "Amen," she said again. Her eyes were like this whenever we would talk about the children we might have had. It is personal and I will not tell it, except to say that I had many seeds and all were aimless as cottonwood and dandelion seeds. If we had had children, I think everything might have been different between us. Childless, we gave less in lovers' love and gave more in friendship love to each other, and I to Frank, and she to Recita.

Cecilia looked calmly around her. "Look at you," she said to me. I was close next to Recita, too close, and I think that was the first Recita and I both knew that my hands were closed inside hers. How did this happen? No matter how, it was all right. Cecilia's eyes said so.

When Frank had first arrived seven hours earlier he had unfolded his short purple stole and placed it on his shoulders. He took the stole off now and his black suit jacket, faded and short in the arms. He draped them over a chair. Recita took them from the chair and folded them, and smoothed them with her hands and stared into them as if to learn something from the cloth.

Cecilia's soul lingered. It would not depart until she received Extreme Unction. Her eyes, ears, nostrils, mouth, hands, and feet were anointed with oil. Frank rested his hand against her forehead and anointed her eyelids with only his thumbnail lightly marking the sign of the cross there. He anointed each ear by holding it in his fingertips and massaging the oil into her earlobes. He pinched her nostrils closed, pressing the oil in deeply. His thumb rocked on her mouth, rocked and made many signs of the cross.

By now, it was late evening, the room was dark, my stomach made noises I could not stop, and when I came back from the kitchen with Ritz crackers and cherry Kool-Aid I wanted to turn on the overhead light. Recita would not allow it. "Don't you dare," she whispered as I brought the first Ritz to my mouth. Her glare would not give permission for even a sip of Kool-Aid, which was in a milkglass pitcher that had been a wedding gift from Elizabeth and Antonio Velasco.

God, more merciful than Recita, gave Frank permission. He drank some of the wine right from the flask. He ate some of the bread. He dipped a piece in wine for Cecilia and fed her once more, as if to invite her soul to linger though he had come to help it depart. He bestowed the Apostolic Blessing and the Plenary Indulgence.

She would not commend her spirit to all the saints and angels. The litany of all of them was said.

"Saint Peter," he said.

"Pray for her," we said.

"Saint Paul."

"Pray for her."

"Saint Andrew." "Saint John." "All ye holy Apostles and Evangelists."

Many saints. They were waiting for Cecilia's soul to enter their company but her soul lingered. Her body shuddered like a hatchling at the bottom of a stream.

"From Thy wrath," he said.

"O Lord, deliver her," we said.

"From an evil death."

"O Lord, deliver her."

Many evils. A long list. She was delivered from them all, but her soul still lingered there. With Frank.

Hours passed. Frank said the Acts of Most Necessary Virtue for the Sick, which he and my mother and Recita had said for Cecilia two weeks earlier. My mother had visited Cecilia often in her last weeks, and she had brought blessings she had not learned from missals. Without saying it, she brought the blessings to Cecilia *and* to Recita.

Frank invited Cecilia to make an Act of Resignation, an Act of Submission, and an Act of Self-Oblation, all the Acts of Most Necessary Virtue. She would not respond in words. And she would not sleep.

Frank's long, desperate prayers were useless. Exhausted, he said, "Cecilia. Dear. Say 'Amen' to all my prayers."

She said, "Amen," but softly. She said, "Amen," but quietly calling. She said, "Amen," but pleading. When she moved her legs and arms, her feet were exposed and part of her breasts. Frank covered her. "Amen," she said, "Amenamenamen" in a way that was not an Act of Resignation, not an Act of Submission. "Amen," she said like a person making a whispered threat inside a smoke ring. An Act of Noncontrition. It was impossible to tell if she wished now to die. She said

"Amen" over and over again, in little cries of joy until her voice left and the sounds she made faded and her breathing began to fail.

Frank put down the small black missal. He sat on the edge of the bed. He kissed the crucifix and placed it on her still lips. He fitted the crucifix into her fingers, rested her hands on her chest, and it was done.

Recita and I kneeled together. She raised our linked hands to her left breast, quietly tapping her heart.

Frank wiped the sweat from his face. He wiped the tears. "The passing-bell," he said.

Recita rose to bring it to him. He took it, but he handed it back so that she could ring it first, and then I could, and he last of all.

Frank had put into his suitcase the passing-bell, the two glasses, spoon, candlestick, and folded cloth. He sat in a corner of the room in shadows that made him smaller and thinner than he already was. He had a handsome face, dimpled at the corners of his mouth and faintly dimpled in the middle of his chin. There was shadow in the lower part of his face, but light reflected off his wide, unwrinkled forehead and his sharp high cheekbones, and his wide, flat nose; and the light in his golden-brown freckles won over the darkness.

In his lap he held the flask and the little bit of remaining bread. "You will cut her hair?" he asked.

Recita nodded yes. Cecilia had asked that Recita borrow the electric clippers of Leo Rascón. A week earlier the cousin of a friend of Leo Rascón's sister had delivered them, and proudly showed Cecilia that he had replaced the batteries, he had brushed clean the mechanisms of this family treasure. He showed her the child's toothbrush he used. He put it back in his shirt pocket. They had no other discussion and said no good-byes.

Recita asked me to sit next to Frank, and she pushed a chair next to him, and guided me into the chair. She brought me the crackers and the white pitcher of Kool-Aid. When Frank ran out of wine, he and I shared the Kool-Aid. When he ran out of bread, we shared the crackers. We watched Recita turn Cecilia's head on the pillow and guide the clippers where they needed to go. She moved her hand over Cecilia's bare scalp then, and brushed the black needles and soft wisps onto the pillow. In a few turns, a few passes of the clippers, she finished. She took away the pillow, turned the pillowcase inside out to hold the hair, and put aside the pillow. She brought a bowl of warm water and hand soap and washed Cecilia's head with a piece of old sponge. She said, "Come," and I came to the bed to see Cecilia. Undisguised truth. Love and Sweetness. Beautiful amen.

Later, before I walked her home, Recita gave me the pillowcase with Cecilia's hair inside so that I could give it to my mother.

I have Cecilia's hair now. I have two hundred and fifty-four packages of hair. Before the end of the month, I will have two hundred and fifty-five or six. The hair that people send me gets lost in the mail sometimes, but it arrives sooner or later. In envelopes, in boxes of all sizes, their spirits come here for my care. Upon their deaths, they send or their families send their hair because they promised my mother they would. I have the hair of Elizabeth and Antonio Velasco, Frank's mother and father. I have the hair of Robert Morales, father of the sheriff.

When she healed them, they paid by promising their hair. From their heads. All of the hair from their heads. She asked nothing else but that she have their hair when they died. To be buried bald—a small price. Some were bald at the funeral service. Some were clipped by a family member afterward.

If you asked why, she asked you back, "Where is your spirit? Have you not seen it?"

And she answered herself, "You have."

And she asked, "What part of you has already died but grows?"

And she answered herself, "Your hair. *El cabello*. The spirit."

I asked about this. How many times I asked, you cannot imagine. What did my hair have to do with my spirit? She said, "When have you ever seen two heads of hair the same?"

She said, "Why the hair? Ask Samson. Ask Delilah."

As far back as I can remember, packages came. She opened them, she spread the heads of hair over the kitchen table. I could not help myself, I would ask again: "This is the spirit?"

"*Es verdad*. A person's thoughts live under it but not inside it."

"Oh, Mother."

"It can be tempered, but not tamed."

"Mother," I said. "What about bald people? Bald babies? Where is their spirit?"

"Their teeth," she said.

"And toothless people?"

"Fingernails. Toenails."

The mail never brought us teeth or nails. She could not heal a person with no hair.

I have my father's hair. I have my mother's hair. I mean, I have them in boxes. In 1973, when she was dying, my mother asked if I would have her hair. I said, "I have healed you of nothing, Mother."

Leo Rascón's sister brought my mother's hair to me the day of her funeral. I have the hair of Leo Rascón.

I have the straight, dull black hair of my wife Cecilia, who died so many years ago. My mother healed Cecilia of her anger at dying so young. Cecilia had made her the promise, and so I have one fistful of Cecilia's fragrant hair.

Maggie Gamboa waited my mother's other tables for her because she, too, was a priestess. She brought me a fried tortilla dusted with cinnamon and sugar. When I gave her back her record book, I watched what cabinet she put the book inside. She asked, "Does the ledger say I am rich?"

"It says you could buy me two radios if you wanted," I said. Although he did not have everything yet, my father had bought most of the makings, different parts each month, for a radio, an Atwater-Kent: the binding posts, the variable condensers, the antenna insulators, antenna wires, detectors, and even the set of Henley Radio books, but not yet the Willard Radio "B" rechargeable storage battery.

"I am that rich?" she asked. How she laughed! Who in our valley does not hear her low, musical coughing laughter even now? She broke off a piece of my *buñuelo* for herself.

I said, "It's mine."

"I made it," she said.

She took more and ate, and said I should go home without my mother, and went back to waiting tables, paying me no attention. No attention at all.

Along the way home I visited my holy place of stolen

things. Here is what I had constructed: a small pretend well, a small tree; I made the huge book serve as a front door for the small pretend house. Two mighty words of greeting: Standard Diary.

At home, my father asked me if I would fry him an egg for dinner, one of Willa Hancock's renter's eggs, which were pale green and the yoke chrome gold, this is no lie, chariot gold, lowrider gold. We heard her renter was an angel who had visited and stayed, an elderly woman angel, that is all I can say. (This happened more in 1924 than it does now.) And her chickens, nine chickens, which the angel brought with her from Kentucky, liked Willa's horses, and rode their backs, and the renter must have been an angel because every clutch of eggs her chicken laid amazed her and amazed the horses and Willa and us. They were green, unwashed, undyed farm eggs— but a different green. They smelled like strong coffee, and when we showed one to Willa's horses they grew quiet. Awed, do you see what I mean?

I fried him one and me one, spilled chopped green chiles over them, some salt and Tabasco. We said grace before we scooped them up with tortillas and folded them once over with our thumbs and once over with our other fingers. Our elbows went out, like this, out and up. We leaned down and levered our wrists and hands to our faces, I and my father. Your rough giant's face was mostly untrimmed red beard, and your eyes never wandered from me, Father. Your green eyes with rusty spokes in them. What did we say to each other?

You said . . .

I said . . .

We didn't say anything, did we? I remember all of the nothing we said. Your wrists were sunburned almost black where your shirtsleeves and work gloves left a gap. Your face was small really, not much chin, not giant. But any man is vast who looks so deeply into his son. Maybe your eyes were only green, not sacred green, I can see that now, but they drew a circle around my face and my own eyes and another circle around something true you found in my eyes that made your smile as fiercely hopeful as a dog biting the fleas on its back.

I was reading the *El Paso Daily Herald* to him when my mother came home. She stood close behind him, put her hands in the tufts of red hair at his neck. I read: "El Paso is to have its first radio dance. A real honest to goodness radio dance, probably the first in El Paso as far as hiring a real dance hall and putting on a dance in first-class fashion is concerned." I read it the way I thought I should. With a clever tone. I mispronounced, and that was a problem, but if an article was melodramatic or sentimental or flat or tough, I could adjust my tone. My tone was good. My parents were proud of how I read.

My mother whispered something to my father—I couldn't hear what.

"Darlin'," he said. "I moved her."

"La Montañita?" she asked. She laughed with delight when he said, "That's the one. Moved her along."

She pulled his neck hairs. She said something playful to him and he said, "No. No, darlin'. It's the truth." I think she had asked if he was lying, because he liked to be a liar sometimes.

I read: "The members of the Original Entre Nous Club of El Paso will stage this last word in dances Saturday, July 10, in the ballroom of the Hutchins Hotel."

My father explained that what he had moved was a great pile of rocks. I guessed that it was his largest pile; he always called it "her." And my mother called it "La Montañita," the little mountain. We always had small mountains of rock on our two acres of land. We had a sign on our flatbed wagon and a sign atop two columns of rough stone:

We Build
GREET Walls

The low rock wall around our land was so perfect Father needed no further proof of or advertising for his artistry.

He said, "The Alcedamas will get her."

"I saw them today!" I said, remembering the Stetson that was not there.

My mother said, "They tip good." Still standing behind him, she put her foot on his knee so he could untie that shoe. He unlaced it. He pushed his fingers under the tongue. With his whole hand, he drew her foot from the shoe. He drew her black cotton stockings over her heel and, slowly, down and off.

She asked me to finish reading the newspaper article "First Radio Dance to Be Given Soon."

I read the last part: "The music will be broadcast from WKY, the El Paso Radio Shop. It is reported that the young ladies are planning favors for their gentlemen friends in the shape of tubes, variocouplers, and magnavoxes."

Only later, when they were both smoking cigarettes, my mother's bare feet in my father's lap and her telling about Mrs. V, did I hear her tell him what she had whispered earlier: "He is hurting her."

My father asked, "How?"

"Words," she said. She closed her eyes as if to remember what words, but only repeated, "Words."

"And the boy too?"

"¿Quién sabe?" she said. "Who knows?" She liked clove cigarettes, to put the filter and her fingertips between her lips, to breathe in and slowly breathe out the smoke. It stained the skin around her chin and mouth.

She is so much to me, my mother, but only so much smoke and breath and handfuls of rag and beat-up big feet and crumbs of word when I tell about her.

My father said, "She'll have to get out then, won't she? And take the boy."

"Where?" my mother asked. "Where would they go?"

63

The Church would not approve. Marriage is a sacrament: to hold the family together, a holy duty. That is what Mrs. V would be told by the One True Faith, and if her husband shouted words, what were they but only words? And because that is how they were taught, her family would tell her the same, and her friends who were, after all, Catholic school friends, would say the same: Holy. Holy. Holy.

"Who can ever help her if heaven isn't on her side?" my father asked.

In heaven all bets are covered, aren't they, Father? You will tell me when I get there, won't you?

You looked into the cigarette smoke, not through it but into it, Father. I could picture your thoughts, could see you running from the One True Faith again, one more time, out of the burning marble and gold Catholic Church, the foundation centuries old, molten and shifting, the stench suffocating, the high church walls crumbling, the doors closed to so many. And I could already imagine you returning, submitting yourself like all the defeated in order to ask forgiveness that you ever fled.

IN
A VISION

On a Saturday night in May 1982, the Bishop asked me to come with Recita to his greenhouse. He wanted to celebrate his tenth anniversary with us, he said. He wanted us to wear old clothes. We would paint.

"Paint?" I asked.

"And bring old toothbrushes," he said.

"Paint? At night?"

He said, "Don't tell anyone."

He was an amazing man. After Cecilia's funeral and burial, when Frank had been made bishop in 1972, there was a High Mass, an endless ceremony, a fiesta, a parade for La Virgen de Guadalupe who had stood in the center of the Christ Is King cemetery for seventeen years. She was carved from Ponderosa pine and cottonwood root by Ajax Ruíz, who said she was so tall and large because of a vision he had in his father's 1939 black Packard on the Feast of Immaculate Conception in 1943, when Ajax was seventeen and a hellraiser. He had a vision but he ignored it, went on being a hellraiser for nineteen years, up to the summer he carved Our Lady. Nine feet tall. La Magnífica. He chopped and carved her robed figure and head and her folded hands and bare feet with his hatchet, exactly as he said he would to anyone who knew about his vision and asked him, What are you waiting for? Another vision?

The statue makes you dizzy with yearning because of the shape of her half-closed eyes and her open lips and her mouth telling secrets, telling secrets. Her hands are giant and rough and her giant feet rougher, a crust of dry skin around her soles, her toes very old and injured. Ajax saw her that way. In a vision. He hollowed her out: body, head, hands, feet. This will not sound strange, I know, except that he hollowed her out so much that her surface, even the surface of her hands and feet, was thin as the skin of a drum.

The Bishop told Recita and me about this that night in his clean, brightly lit, new greenhouse, a place he cherished because of his love for gardening—and for hellraisers. This windowed house was built for him by the Christ Is King youth group, his own group of churchgoing ex-gangbangers. They caused talk. They—over twenty of them—boys, girls, grown women and men—got their heads shaved, got indigo blue crowns of thorns tattooed completely around their heads, grew their hair back. (The Bishop's "official" defense of them? "Christ's Pirates," he said.)

Recita and I wiped Our Lady's body with dry rags, and we turned her on her side and back and front in order to miss nothing on her. We saw her. We saw her hands, how carefully Ajax had made the deep lines inside her palms, a cursive *F* in the left palm and a reverse *F* in the right palm. We saw how broad her shoulders were and how wide her back and hips, and realized we did not know her though we had thought we knew her well. We had come to the cemetery and prayed to her about Cecilia. About us. We had confided in Our Lady many times. We had felt consoled by her. And now we were old, and emptied of many kinds of desire, and filled with new kinds, and to touch her was an honor so dear it made it impossible for me to have impure thoughts as we removed grit and dust from her waist and breasts and her smooth neck. Is a huge woman purer than a small one? Remembering, I am impure in my thoughts again. I have a soul of hard-packed dung.

Without touching the statue, the Bishop supervised, asking that we clean her red gown better, each fold, and then asking that we strip the paint from her blue mantilla. The original paint.

Recita asked, "How will we match the colors?"

"We won't," said the Bishop.

Borrowing his orator's voice, I said, "Of course we won't," which made Recita frown at me in the way she might frown at a man in a hospital bed who deserved her sympathy but should not make himself pitiful.

We stripped the thick blue paint—maybe seven layers— and found beneath it Ajax's hidden devotion in how lovingly he made the wood become flowing cloth and how humbly he hid his art beneath the color. "It seems impossible," I said. Recita asked, "How? How?"

"Knives and spoons," said the Bishop, who believed there must be the right tools for the right miracles. "Ajax had no carving tools. He wasn't a sculptor, not even a woodcarver. So?" His own question excited him. "So. His hatchet found her image in the wood. He sharpened table knives and spoons. Scooped. Scraped. Hundreds of hours, for three years."

We sanded, Recita and I. We blew grit from the surface of the wood and smiled secretly at each other, not knowing the Bishop saw our delight and our pleasure. He asked, "Do I have something I should do?" He answered himself, "Yes! I'll be right back." He went out the greenhouse door with the dustpan of dirt and grit he had swept. And he didn't come back.

He knew about us. He knew how long we had wanted— ten years since Cecilia's death—to pass our breaths and hands and fingers together in prayerfulness over old surfaces. He had given himself the gift of offering us this gift.

Recita said, "Where has he gone?" Our faces were close

to the wood, and when she said it we could hear the word "gone" return.

I said, "Away." She said, "At last!" and all of it came back from within Our Lady: *Away—at last*. We laughed. She laughed.

"Like a giant flute," I said.

Recita said, "We have whispered our secrets to her and now she is telling."

"No," I said, "she's laughing."

"That's worse," Recita said. I could have said, "That's better," but Recita would have frowned.

Leaning so our faces were very close, we brushed her dusky face with our toothbrushes, taking away every trace of grit from her open mouth and lips and eyes. I wanted, waited to be kissed. A man is supposed to want to kiss, I know, I know, and will only be embarrassed if he waits to be kissed. I waited. Recita waited, wanted—any ass could see this. If it is true that innocence inspires lust, then lust inspires innocence, I guess. We fell silent. We fell innocent. For another hour we fell back to our work.

Our Lady's hands and face and neck glistened from the spit on our toothbrushes. When we cleaned her poor flat feet we saw how beaten Ajax had made them and how the elements had warped them. Recita had just kissed them when the Bishop came in carrying three or four of his best bishop's robes. He threw them on the floor.

"Kissing, eh?" he said. He touched the top of our foreheads with his hands and pressed in to see how soft our brains had gotten, I suppose, or how much of our fever he could feel in his palms. "Is she ready?" he asked me.

Recita and I nodded yes, more or less shaking our heads free from his hands. Recita said, "Ajax was a great artist."

"Inspired!" said the Bishop. "Never carved before then. Never carved again." He touched Our Lady's whole neck, circling it with his fingers. He tapped the front of her newly cleaned throat. He rapped it with a knuckle and said, "I have a wood saw," and said, "a good one," and said, "Here—almost at her shoulders, we will saw off her head."

"Lord!" I said.

"Why?" asked Recita, resting her hands on my hands, which rested on Our Lady's feet.

He had lifted the saw from a nail on the wall only two feet behind him. He said, "She must be facedown."

"Why?" Recita took her waist, and gave me the signal, and we turned her. "Okay," she said, "tell why."

He didn't answer.

Gripping Our Lady's left shoulder in his left hand, he sawed with his other by pushing forward and rocking the blade up so the teeth farthest from the handle ripped and nearest the handle cut. When her head came off, he passed it to me. I passed it to Recita, who looked inside and asked, "What now?"

An hour later, around eleven o'clock, we had finished cutting up his robes and stuffing the long pieces inside the statue. We had used hanger wires to push strips into the hands and feet. We had stirred the three gallons of red paint and the three gallons of white paint, the only paint the Bishop—who had forgotten paintbrushes—had bought. He said, "Lieutenant Galván. Do you remember him, Red? His son Cleophas, a young man then, brought this paint for me from Jalisco—all that way. He went because I sent him." The Bishop's own power to request the impossible or the absurd always amazed him. He chuckled. "Cleophas is a good man. A good man with a faith too strong to ask questions."

Recita asked, "Is that a good faith—to never ask questions?"

The Bishop held his breath a second. He hummed. There was a conversation going on between him and God. I knew him so long that I knew this. He put his stirrer into the red paint and looked into it, and God looked into it too, and the Bishop stirred. He said, "I say stupid things too often, and I should not be bishop."

I am not ashamed of what we did. Recita is not ashamed. Not now. But at the time, as we glued Our Lady's head on, Recita whispered, "A sin!" and the words echoed back at all three of us. For a long time after that Recita said, "You two drew me in." Whenever the Bishop heard our confessions, she blamed him and cursed him behind the closed curtains of the confessional, and he begged her forgiveness again.

Sometimes now Recita will hold up her two arms before me, and smile, and I know she is showing me how her hands and arms up to the elbows were covered in white paint that night, and mine too, and the Bishop's, because he had not brought paintbrushes. We painted her with our hands and fingers, like children will do.

When the white, white Virgen de Guadalupe—white robes, white face and hands, blinding white, beaten, ancient feet—was returned to her place in the Christ Is King cemetery on August 15, the Feast of the Assumption, some wanted to change her back. Some wanted to hide her. Some wanted to know how we would ever know that she was Mexican. Everyone wondered: How could this happen? What does it mean? And everyone waited for answers, which were never given. They were never given.

Two years later, there were items in our newspaper: "Witnesses Questioned about Miracle Statue," "Pilgrims Come from Around the World," "Bishop Amazed."

From 1983 to 1986 she perspired blood which worked miracles in the lives of those who touched it, and there is no doubt of that. Go and see the hundreds of home-drawn and handwritten accounts put down on hammered tin and laid at her feet. A necklace of red formed at her throat, and when rain came, this red blood made her white gown rose-pink, though

her mantilla remained white. From 1986 on, she became suf-
fused with darkening moistness. It made her glisten. In her
palms the *F*s filled with this dark blood, and it dripped from
her fingers on that Good Friday. Slowly, she became one coppery red color from her head to her feet. Awe-inspiring feet.

Another item, a front-page headline, appeared in newspapers all over New Mexico and Texas: "Wonders Investigated."

The first time we made the buttered bread and lemonade for the Velascos, my father asked, "What in the Lord's Name do you think you are doing?"

My mother explained that we must forgive my father for being a man and forever doomed to ask questions. "You are half a man," she said to me. "This is half as bad as being a whole man, and half of half as bad as being like your father."

Before our own dinner, we took the buttered bread and lemonade to the Velascos. Mr. V liked the lemonade strong and unsugared, his bread buttered to the very edges and folded like a document. His wife had told my mother this and warned that he would not accept charity, which my mother said would not matter because God was involved now.

We knocked at the door of their home, a two-room hut. My mother stood on the footpath several steps behind us where the single green cane of a century plant had rocketed up from one to twenty feet high in only two months. I held our offering up.

Mr. V said, "My wife told me you would come."

"Good," said my mother.

Mr. V asked, "What is this?"

"Gifts," said my father.

"What?"

"Gifts, dammit." It was not what my mother had told him he must say.

Francisco at his side, Mr. V glared at us, touching his son on the arm, drawing him near him. You could see Francisco unriddle us all at once, and try to lean forward out of the trap of his father's arms. For a fifteen-year-old boy, he was small. He was so much smaller than Mr. V. Mr. V stepped back, tenderly drew him nearer, tried to read our faces. Then he looked instead at his son. "Are you all right?" he asked Francisco, who did not answer. "A good boy," said Mr. V. He slammed the door.

After the splintering sound of the wooden door against its frame, there was no other sound on earth, none.

Leaving, we heard the seams of one sewn-together word give way. "Youbitchyoubitchyoubitch." We heard the tearing sounds of other words, the almost joyful, vicious ripping cry a vulture makes.

"We will eat here," my mother said, not ten yards from the hut.

"That I won't do," said my father.

"Me neither," I said.

"Yes. You will. *Siéntense. Here,*" she said, this last word buried to its head in one hammerstrike.

My father held up two questions: the pitcher and the plate.

"There," she said, and he set them there.

We sat down in the hot dirt near the century plant. Its eight flowering branches, growing only at the top, were like some impossible candelabra lit by the sky's blue fire. My mother raked ants off the ground around us, her palm making table-cleaning arcs.

"We should eat," she said.

We could not. Not eat. Not talk.

73

My father looked into the pitcher. "What've you done to this lemonade?"

She explained that she had said a prayer into the pitcher, a different prayer was inside the folded pieces of bread. We could eat, it was okay, the prayers wouldn't harm us, she said. But the prayers she had recited into that pitcher of bitterness were *words,* and I confess I couldn't have been more afraid of such words if they had been pounded into my hands and feet.

The wind in Mr. V's shouts spread fire far beyond the hut. The hut door flung open and Francisco ran out, choking and gasping, rolling himself in the dirt as if to put out cinders burning over him. He hummed, "Hmmm, hmmmm, hmmm-mmm," like he always did all his life.

We watched him, pathetic watchers, our shoulders hunched up and our hands anchored in the dirt where the ants could climb us. "Francisco," I said, "over here."

My father pulled Francisco down to him, held the lemonade up to his mouth. Francisco was ashamed to drink this way. He took the glass. He gulped, his muddy mouth and closed eyes trembling.

I said, "Give him some bread."

My mother said, "Not yet."

She asked him, a few minutes later, to raise a piece of bread with both hands over his head and draw it down like a knife. Francisco knew what she meant. In our valley, the tradition in bad storms that might damage crops was to have a child raise a knife and draw it down through the air in order to cut the storm.

Francisco looked at me for some kind of okay sign.

I said, "Why not?"

My mother put the bread in his hands. I asked, "Are there words he's got to say?"

She shook her head no. Her hands hovered over his, her fingers curved up and then fluttered away.

He raised up the folded piece of bread. He seemed to know what part of the air he wished to cut open.

After he cut the air, less shouting came from the hut. By then, Mr. V was tired, I guess. Francisco cut again. He cut again. He cut again. He ate the knife made of bread.

My mother gave me one of the pieces of bread, gave my father the other. She offered us the lemonade, which we gulped, and she gave the rest to Francisco, who drank. And hummed.

Frank. Should a dark Mexican—a mestizo—have had as many freckles as you had? Unfolded freckled wings under your eyes—they made amazement seem to have always just landed on your face. You rubbed and wept them pale and even your laughter eroded those freckles, but I see, I see them now, Frank, and miss you, your beauty. Should one man admit to such longing for another man's beauty?

We had to leave you there. You did not know how my father cried quietly when we left. He felt like a coward. To find a child in the darkness, undig him from it, and bury him in it again: cowardly.

My mother said to him, "God is involved now, *mi querido*."

He said that maybe the Velascos only needed money, he knew how having nothing makes you want to stab at the emptiness. Maybe they needed good clothes and food, he said, he must get them some. "And did you see their shack?" he asked. "It's hardly a rug and a roof." I might have said that it was as much as we had. I might have said that, but he would not have seen how that mattered to me.

He pushed his hands through his hair and shot them up above the peak of his head. "By God and the grace of the saints, I'll make this stop."

I will have to tell more about his hair. At another time, I will tell about his hair.

One thing. When Frank was a young priest and he brought my father the last sacraments so many years later, my father would not ask forgiveness for having forsaken the Church. He apologized, instead, for his hair, which was long and stank and was not ready for heaven. "And will he really go to heaven?" I asked right in front of my father.

"He will go there ugly," Frank said, and he never said anything wiser.

HYSSOP

The People's dreams. They cross so many rivers and fences, and they migrate to the chile fields from heaven itself. I can touch only the hem of such dreams.

I told this to Recita after the evening church service, after I watched the People receive communion. They had come right from the fields to Christ Is King church.

I said, "Everything that is ours will be theirs and ours."

Recita said to me, "Red, since when does *el espanta pára-jos* philosophize?"

"All scarecrows philosophize," I said. "We scare you away, then we are alone to do our thinking."

She let me walk her home, but not hold her hand. I already knew I had no permission to hold her hand until we were two blocks away from the church. "*Now*, old woman?" I asked.

"Now," she said, and her fingers moved over my hand and opened it as if to make the clay of me become a bowl. "You have changed, no, Red Greet?"

"No," I said, but we both knew better, so this was our joke.

"No?" she said. Grinned.

Younger people do not say they love each other in these ways, do they? For the older ones, surrendering is dearer. Hearing, healing, remembering, forgetting, are dearer.

At her door, I was allowed to kiss her face below her left eye, tasting the old tears. She kissed me inside my hand, her face so deep inside that my fingers could touch her forehead.

"Go home," she said.

On my way home I passed the Bishop's empty house. I walked across his unweeded but beautiful gardens to the small greenhouse behind his house. I tried the emerald-green door-knob, rattled the door, which would not open. I sat with my back against the bright yellow door, and my knees grew stiffer, and I held them in my arms.

I often drove Eusebio's new LeBaron to Recita's apartment, and parked it there so Recita and I could walk to church together. After Mass, I drove it home—to Eusebio's home. I was the guardian. I guarded Eusebio's home and land in Atocha, which is between Radium Springs and Las Almas. I lived in his rooms, read his books and magazines, his newspaper, adjusted the tone of the faces on his three color televisions right. "Watch": that was my job description. You could have given his place and his possessions a whole map dot on the map of New Mexico, there was so much he owned.

I, who had once stolen money from Eusebio, had been welcomed into his home. I, Red Greet, had been made the guardian of his wealth because he, a successful motel owner, was a greater sinner than I. This, I think, is a miracle: I have been assigned less penance for seventy-five years of stealing people's possessions than Eusebio has been assigned for not sharing his wealth on *one night* when he was visited by people in need. Is this not a miracle? It is. Everything I tell I tell in order to testify to miracles. And to ask absolution.

A thief makes a good guard. All that you own, the thief knows the value of it better than you do.

Eusebio and me. A partnership. I did not allow trespasses against us, nor forgive them. I flashed my flashlight, I called the police, I fired a gun into the air. If I needed to, I sent Eusebio's two yappy toy hell-poodles out to terrorize any crow who sought a place to land, or any dove who tried to take away the smallest branch.

One night the Bishop came unannounced. You see, he worried about my soul and me alone with each other in Eusebio's home, and so, he visited sometimes. But usually he phoned first.

This one night I am telling about, I shot in the air because he came when I was philosophizing, talking to myself deep inside myself, and I heard something trying to break into my unprotected mind. I did not know it was the Bishop in the darkness of Eusebio's fields.

"*Hola!*" he said, a happy voice shot straight at me. I fired into the sky. Twice.

He stepped onto the wide back patio. He held open his Albertson's Superstore jacket to look at himself, like he wanted to see his own wounds before he would believe. "Red," he said, a big grin on his face, "I am ready for heaven, but I would like to go without leaks in me."

We both looked. He had no leaks, praise God. "You are not skinny," I said. "I could make you skinny with my gun."

He took the Colt and my flashlight, and shined light on me, over all of my body, slowly blessing me with it the way someone is blessed in incense.

"I'm hungry," I said.

"Still?"

"Always." Why did I confess this? I thought he saw my hunger.

He turned the flashlight off and on. Through the darkness, moonlit dust whirled. The sweat on the Bishop's face
glittered. We watched the dust spin in the breath of the night,
and said nothing.

He turned off the flashlight. "I must do something," he
said. He hummed, sadness escaping from him. He turned the
flashlight on, pointed the light down. He made conversation
with the toes of his shoes. Bishop shoes. One shoe close to the
other; black, resoled lace-ups. "I will," he said. "I will bless the
chile festival tomorrow. In Hatch."

"Good. Why not?" I said, but I knew this saddened him,
of course it did, to bless the great open-air hangar and, under
it, the farm owners and many others he had fought with about
the migrant children working in the fields. And the housing.
And the pay. And the short hoe, which injured young spirits,
old backs.

I asked, "Frank, why are you here? So late?"

He looked down at the fine patio bricks. Expensive,
glazed brick, and laid in an L pattern. "I was praying," he said.
"I was asking God—for an answer. And I came here. Imagine!"
Why should such joy ring from him in that darkness? I don't
know. The good mysteries are holy mysteries.

He pointed the gun into the air. He pointed it at the red
chile fields and at Eusebio's mansion and toward Atocha as if
he looked down the barrel at long train tracks or into or out of
a deep grave. He pointed it at me, and because I had less faith
than the Bishop, I said, "Give me that!"

He gave me the gun.

"It is very late," I said. "Do bishops sleep?"

"Too much," he said, and then he asked, "Why am I
here?" repeating it, a broken record. He was praying, I figured,
for all real prayer begins with that question. He said, "I have
come here to ask you to answer my prayers, Red."

"Me?" I asked, touching my chest, the starched, new cotton of Eusebio's shirt, which fit me but did not suit me.

In Eusebio's living room, drinking his wine, we became pirates, according to the Bishop's plan.

So. His plan. He said he would commandeer his own home and land, owned by the diocese. I would commandeer Eusebio's home.

Me casa es su casa, people say who never mean it. *My home is your home.* The migrant families would move into Eusebio's and the Bishop's homes every chile and onion season, that was the Bishop's plan.

"For always?" I asked.

"Permanent!" he said.

"Is it against the law?"

"Whose law?" he asked. "God's law?"

"We should get more wine," I said, and I brought us two red bottles from the wine rack, which was in the kitchen closet, secret and dark and cold as the confessional. A whole closet of wine—can you picture this?—two hundred, three hundred bottles. If we pirated his home, when Eusebio returned in November from his pilgrimage to Mexico he would see bottles missing, his doors unlocked, parts of his chile fields made into gardens, his goats, chickens, ducks out of their pens, and children crowding every room, adjusting the tone on his televisions, running his clean water into his polished tubs, reading the words in his books, teasing his guard poodles guarding nothing anymore. I could picture it. But, I confess this, I did not believe it would happen. Oh, I went along with the Bishop that night. I helped him build the whole idea. You know how this is. You cast your net and wait, but you expect emptiness. You carry Christ's cross a little way up the hill, but you hand it back. You build an ark, but you do not believe the flood will come. You send out the crow, but you wait to send out the dove.

In a few hours, we had not had too much wine, this is the truth. One bottle. I said, "So. We take Eusebio's land, just take it? He will be surprised!"

"Why?" asked the Bishop. He was trying to lace up his shoes, which he had taken off. He tried again, no success. (Okay, I confess this, we drank too much wine. Two bottles. Three.) The Bishop asked, "Why should Eusebio be surprised? He knows you are a thief."

I never take offense at the truth. "And what about you?" I said. "*You* are a *bishop*."

"See," he said, or he said, "*Sí*," or "She." I think he said, "*Sí*." He laughed at his unlaced shoes, left them unlaced. "Shame on them if they are surprised!" he said. "A criminal. A bishop. Same thing. Nothing we have is ours."

A scapular on a black string fell out of the Bishop's white shirt and he could not get it back in. We laughed at this. Weak and helpless laughter. We sat in stuffed vinyl recliners across from each other. In a band across the center of his face, the Bishop had the faint wings of a butterfly made of freckles, very faint. When we were boys, I remember he could almost make the skin of his face fly by opening his eyes very wide.

We spoke of Recita. The Bishop had many opinions about Recita and me, he said. "I see you during the Mass. You sing to each other. It is like watching a bad musical."

I said, "I have confessed too much to you."

The Bishop said, "Too much? I think you have held back."

The arms of my recliner were far away from my arms. I was like a child in God's lap. I had so much room to move, and yet I could not move. "I am ashamed," I said.

"I see. Cecilia? Cecilia." The Bishop hummed. Solemn

humming. "Red," he said, "it was twenty-two years ago. She was dying. Halfway into heaven, and closing the gate to this life behind her. Hand me the bottle."

I explained that I couldn't escape my chair.

"No?" He shifted, grunted. "*Dios!*" he said. "I can't move either!"

The vinyl of our recliners made a kind of squeaking conversation while we were silent. I thought of how I courted Recita in the church, my wife Cecilia already becoming an angel. What do you call new angels? She was becoming a faint whisper, a memory, a spirit. She said to me, once when I returned from the church, she said, "You will be all right, Red. Look at you. You are a man with a river inside." She was becoming a breeze, a bright grain of salt. She seemed pleased for me, and amazed by me.

I said to the Bishop, "I crossed the line—with Recita."

He chuckled when he tried again to leave his recliner. He settled in. "Weird!" he said, with real joy. He said, "You have sinned, Red. You have asked for absolution and you have been absolved, I know, because I myself absolved you. The last day I forgave your sins was probably a bad stomach day for me. My stomach hates every food I love, you know. I thought—I think—what was I saying?"

"You were saying adultery is okay."

"Was I? Adultery? I am one pathetic bishop."

"Any more pathetic and you could be the Pope," I said.

We must have fallen asleep laughing. In my dreams I heard hungry purring in the dark, cold den where I had been thrown by the Pharaohs or the IRS—this was a dream, so I couldn't be sure. I was dancing with a man. Intimate. My companion in the den said, "Praise God!" over and over.

I never talk in my sleep. In my dreams I cannot talk, or I would have said, "Be quiet."

Noise in the room woke me. It was early in the morning, before sunrise. The Bishop said, "Red. Did you know this chair will massage you?" He turned the switch on, which made the recliner and the Bishop purr. "Praise God!" he said.

I said, "Okay. Praise God. Why not?" I had a burning headache on the peak of my head.

"See what time it is?" I showed him my watch, Eusebio's watch really, which had a small light inside. Four A.M.

"The festival! I should leave," the Bishop said. "I must not be late." His black shoes clomped across the room. I followed him out of the house.

Glittering dust lapped in small waves over the patio bricks we walked across. When I fell, he said, "Get up. Follow me."

I asked, "Why?" but I followed.

We strode through a row of ripe red chile plants in the chile field. I could barely see him. He moved deeper into darkness. He said, "God will give signs."

"Why not?" I said, confident no signs would come, that God would never go along with any of it.

"Have a little faith," he said.

"I better—I should—I have to go back," I said.

He asked, "Do you trust God?"

"Well. God knows I have a headache. I trust there is a reason."

"You don't trust enough," he said. "Look, Red, will you just meet me at the festival?"

I agreed to 7 A.M.

Eusebio's aspirin and his shower and his reclining chair and coffee were, again, mine alone. But I do not believe these healed my headache.

I closed my eyes. They traveled me over every part of Eusebio's map dot, his smooth quilt of land near Fort Selden where black soldiers were once under the command of Major MacArthur, the father of the more famous one, the General.

Eusebio's acres of orderly pecan trees seemed to march one generation behind another. The youngest trees were far away; the oldest trees, closest to his home. Esther's Produce Stand is only just across the highway, which is on the path Don Juan Oñate rode almost four hundred years ago. Brooding over it all is the Sentinel Peak, which had been the troops' lookout post for Indian raids. You can see, this land was the eagle's and the eagle's prey before it was the Indians'. It was the Conquistadors' before it was the priests', and the conquerors' sons' before it was the Mexicans', and the Mexicans' before it was the Texans', and the new settlers' before it was the troops', and the settlers' sons' and the bankers' as soon as it was the miners' and the railroaders', and the farmers' as soon as it was the herders', and the Law's as soon as it was the Outlaws' and then the Law's again, and many, many settlers' and sellers' and buyers' before it was Eusebio's or the place where Esther put up a produce stand under an old cottonwood. The Río Grande is crooked here where it has claimed land and returned it and reclaimed it many times.

My eyes cooled slowly, like heated metal, like loaves of bread. They cooled and they grew smaller as they cooled, and, this is the truth, everything I carried in them, everything I guarded, shrank. I owned nothing, and so I owed nothing. And this healed me. If you believe being healed from a hangover is no miracle, you have never had a hangover.

When I opened my eyes again, I said this vow to myself: "Yes. Yes. Yes."

I asked myself: Do you? Will you? Can you?

To every holy, thieving idea of that night with the Bishop, I said, "Yes."

Under the Hatch Chile Festival hangar the judges made their final decisions, agreed again that the Burgoa and Castillo families, the wealthiest in our valley, should win Best Big Jim,

Best Pequín, Best Barker, Naki, Sandía, Yellow Hat, and Jalapeño. Best everything. "What else can we do?" said the Judge of Judges, who was also the festival emcee and who in real life was a judge, so he knew about me. He had sentenced me to five days once.

The annual chile festival, you see, has sponsors. They are the hosts of the event. The Growers Association, the University Extension Service, the FFA. Many hosts. Many cashboxes from which I had once taken money, too much to go unnoticed. A long time ago.

The judges, in official shiny blue vinyl vests, put out the ribbons. Teófilo Baquiera, who wrote so pretty and had the special pens, wrote the names of all the Chosen on the ribbon tags and then on a posterboard.

The Judge of Judges, whose vest was gold-colored, asked, "Red, why are you here?"

"I am friend to the Bishop," I said. I waved to Frank, who in his full robes and miter and with his staff, looked like a very stylish pirate.

"Mmmm-hm," said the Judge of Judges.

The Bishop waved hello to me.

Only a dozen people were there at all because it was so early in the morning. A good thing.

The Judge of Judges told the Bishop, "Go ahead, do your blessing," but he was not paying attention, no one was.

The Bishop ascended to the stage microphone on the raised concrete platform. He tapped it with his staff, switched it on. He raised his arms up at the corrugated roof, and looked out over the empty folding chairs, and the concession booths all around the open-air hangar, and the dirt strip that would be full of cars soon, and the farmlands that had birthed so many years of festival. Rays of sun made streams of light break over the jagged crown of the Sierra de la Soledad east of us.

"Look," he said, speaking to me. I saw. A sign, hand-drawn. It said,

Corn

Dollar

Ear

The sign was big, ten by ten feet. Why was it so big unless the sign was a Sign? So much space for three words.

The Bishop laughed out loud. He said into the microphone, "I am ready." He hummed.

I heard him. I think I was the only one.

His arms reached very high. Like the face of a man staring into a bonfire, his face was glowing with heat and brightness. He prayed: "May God bless and damn this festival where God's first fruits have been harvested for some good people and denied to other good people.

"May God make an ark for the poor, send a flood for the greedy." He declaimed the words as he had been taught to declaim by Miss Iffrig, one of our teachers seventy years ago.

I was distracted by the sign. Corn Dollar Ear. A word-inkblot-riddle, a what-is-wrong-with-this-picture puzzle. *Ear.* *Ear* was wrong. I had heard so many times in church, "Faith cometh by hearing." Ear Dollar Corn, Ear Corn Dollar, I said to myself.

The Bishop was really worked up. "May God bring the rainbow to this place," he declaimed, "but offer us no promises.

"May God punish but forgive us, make us a chosen people with no chosen land until we choose to share."

I heard him loud and clear. If faith cometh by hearing, then Corn Dollar Ear could be unriddled, simple enough. Food Money Faith. It *was* a sign.

"May God feed and clothe us and starve and strip us naked before each other."

He lowered his arms. "I have an announcement," he said,

and he explained his plan to claim Eusebio's and the Bishop's homes and lands for the children and families of the migrant laborers. In Spanish, in a miraculous number of slowly pronounced syllables, he said, "I claim these lands and properties and all these peoples in the name of Christ Our Lord, the King."

History is a great sin. Time has proven this. Everyone has a different version of what the Bishop said. No one thinks he damned anyone or anything. In the paper was his picture and these words, nothing else:

The Most Reverend Francisco Velasco, C.S.B., D.D., Bishop of the Diocese of Las Almas, blesses the 1994 Annual Hatch Chile Festival.

Afterward, we drove together to Christ Is King church, which is no simple church since it is the cathedral of our diocese. At the church service, Recita sang the longing songs. "Make Me a Channel of Your Peace," she sang, and her longing was another kind of sacred, do you see what I mean?

The time in our lives was changing, and the long shadows of our guilt were maybe retreating, retreating a little.

Recita and I had been in love before our souls gave permission. When my wife was dying, when I was in the church every morning praying for a miracle to heal her or an answer as to why she would not heal, Recita, old good friend, prayed with me. And sang. Always, Recita's singing had been beautiful. It became—how horrible and wonderful this is to say— more angelic the closer my wife came to heaven.

Recita had come to our home for the Holy Viaticum. She was Cecilia's lifelong best friend, and that was her reason for being there. But I had kneeled too close to Recita, too close.

"*Asperges me, Domine, hyssopo, et mundabor: lavabis me, et super nivem dealbabor,*" the priest recited. Thou shalt sprinkle me, O Lord, with hyssop, and I shall be cleansed: Thou shalt wash me, and I shall be made whiter than snow.

I was sixty-two then. Recita was sixty-one.

The second morning of the festival the Bishop came to give another blessing and damning. We submitted the backs of our hands to the old lion at the gate who stamped us APPROVED so we could go inside. When the Judge of Judges asked the two officers on duty to prevent the Bishop from coming inside the hangar, Sheriff Morales asked, "What has this man done?"

During the bless-damning I had sat in a folding chair and drawn a small pirate flag for the Bishop and one for myself. Very beautiful. The flag was a grinning skull and a crossbones at the feet of La Virgen de Guadalupe, whose nose I could not get right because I never practiced drawing noses, but also because I didn't know how it looked, Our Lady's nose. I pinned my pirate flag over the front of my Diablos baseball hat, but he would not wear his. He admired his flag, and said, "Red! The light in Our Lady's face!"

I explained about how many times I had to erase her nose, and that is why the paper was burnished there.

"I *will* wear this!" he said, and drew out his scapular of Christopher, Ex-Saint, and unknotted the black string, threading it through the paper flag. He dropped all of it back under his clothes.

After he put his robes and staff and pirate-bishop's miter in his cherried '82 Monte Carlo lowrider, we walked on the newly graded and tarred highway to the viaduct north of the festival where some of the migrant families had camped, the ones who could not find housing. There were about eight families and twenty to thirty others. The Bishop stood in the center of the highway under the viaduct, and introduced himself. From respect, many of them looked up. They looked away then. He watched them. He probably did not mean to, but he hummed. He looked at his bishop's shoes, at the black road under him. Without raising his voice, he told them his and Eusebio's homes and lands were theirs. "These are yours," he said. "Always yours." His eyes opened wide.

"Beautiful," I said, very private, not wanting anyone to hear. What would they think of one man calling another beautiful? It would be unwise.

They did not believe the Bishop. They did not trust. An angel of the Lord visited them, they heard His voice, but their hearts were hardened.

He repeated that his and Eusebio's homes and lands were theirs. God claimed these places for them, he said.

They ignored him.

We left.

Under the festival hangar, we ate burritos at the Gamboa Burro booth. We talked about the Plan.

"Take your car up the hill," I said. "Let them see your car." The Monte Carlo had been a Christ Is King youth group project. Angels cruise heaven in such chariots. Wet-look wild-cherry paint over a silver base. A pink neon underbelly. On the hood: an airbrushed pearl and turquoise stained-glass cathedral window. Blinding new chrome grille and trim: Epic radials and triple-gold Daytons.

Later in the morning, we went up the hill together. Without the car. We walked until we came to the crowd of workers and their families. The Bishop introduced himself again, as if he did not see most of them in church all the time during the working seasons, did not know their faces and names, give them communion once a week or more. He was afraid, and so he acted official, that is what I think.

A man named César, not *the* César, César Chávez, but a man with *the* César's humble, dangerous eyes, interrupted the Bishop, who was reminding the crowd of women and men and children that they were his flock, he their shepherd. Insulting.

The Bishop was a great and holy man, but he was a Catholic.

"You will lead us?" César said.

"Red and I—" said the Bishop. His voice was shaky. "Red and I will lead—and you, César."

The children crouched under the shadows of the viaduct. The women and the men and teenagers stood in the brightness to which they were more accustomed than the Bishop. Their shoulders and waists were bent in such a way as to make shadows across their own bodies, and in these they were soothed. I wanted to touch them, to be touched by them.

"We need a sign," said César. "*Una buena señal.*" He looked forty or fifty. Ears small and far back on his head, a small head and clever in the quick way it moved. With his black hair mowed to stubble and the tough skin of his temples so shiny he looked like a grackle.

They needed a sign. I was thinking. *Corn Dollar Ear!* But what could I say? Look. Corn. Dollar. Ear. Holy Trinity! No. No. No. I could not say that.

A child, four or five years old, asked a foolish question then. She said this in a voice like a cane tapping a rock—she said it almost too quietly to be heard above the light, warm breeze: "Who you are?"

Dust whispered across bare feet, whispered and hushed. "Who I am?" the Bishop asked. "Mercy!"

A young woman bowed down to the child and pursed her lips in a warning. The child looked through her at the Bishop.

"Who you are?" the child asked.

He didn't answer. I think he couldn't answer.

She asked again. You could see in her concentration on him that the question mattered. She walked to his side. She set one hand over his, like a latch. When she held his other the same way, the tears flowed out of him. "Who am I," he said, and he made ugly boulders with his wrinkled, old fists that he pushed against his face. The tears poured over them.

I made the sign of the cross. Father, Son, and Holy Spirit. "Who am I?" I asked God, the first time I ever prayed this way, trying to cross myself over to God but drowning in words: *Father Dollar Food Money Corn Son Ear Spirit Faith*. And I asked myself, "Who am I?" Any thief knows that all prayer begins with the question "Why am I here?" But I did not know until that moment it ends always with "Who am I?"

This child who asked the question captured my hand. The instant she touched me the tears flowed from me. You understand, I hope: these tears had waited. How long they had waited.

She had knotted the arms of a man's white shirt around her head and under her long hair at the back. She must have swiped her nose with her hand for there was dirt across and underneath it.

Already, the Bishop was answering her question. Here is how he was answering her question: He was undressing! His black shoes and thin black socks already gone. His shirt fallen on the ground behind him.

And now, down came his pants and boxers, yellow as marigolds. In the dust.

To kiss a bishop's ring—this is very private. But to see a bishop's privates is another thing.

I looked. César and all the men and women looked. The children stayed in the shadows, but they stared. You would not?

"I have left the tomb," he said, as Lazarus said, who came naked from his own grave.

We could hear the festival crowd, five or six hundred people. They were noisy like goats chasing goats. Our silence made the goat noises clearer and clearer. I thought I could—I could—understand the flooding and eroding words. We all could. We heard and understood each word though all the words were spoken all at once.

I would need a thousand hours for that five minutes we heard. And we saw like eagles. What we saw right before us!

Frank was naked except for the Piratess of Guadalupe scapular and the scapular of Ex-Saint Christopher, Patron Saint of Ex-Saints. This was all Frank wore.

César, too, had already started to undress, and he stared at me in such a way as to command a miracle. Well, I ask you, what could I do? I undressed.

César kept his shoes on. He had no socks. He wore nothing else. When he whispered to Frank, Frank put his socks and shoes back on.

What set us in motion, this lost tribe of God's unchosen people?

A miracle did.

I did.

I hate seeing a story end before the story's whale swallows someone or spits him out. I said in Spanish, "We should march into the hangar—over there," and I pointed at the festival.

César repeated my words.

Frank said, "We must!"

I said, "We should take all the food we want from the food stands."

Frank said, "I don't think we should—" But César shouted my words to the crowd. The children and the teenagers cheered.

I said, "And all the new quilts and pottery and boots, good boots and shoes, and the clothing, the hand-sewn and embroidered clothes, all we need we should take."

César said to Frank, "This angel is Lucifer!" and he laughed as he repeated my words to everyone. I know this: I know they would not have agreed to any of it without César announcing my words like God had chiseled them for him on stone tablets.

"We should take as much as we need," I repeated. You can see I spoke in Prophetese, the Biblical Words my nakedness inspired in me.

We walked down the steep hill of the highway where the mesquite and devil's claw and thistle and jimson had been scraped away and burned. I carried my clothes and Frank's and César's in an Albertson's plastic bag. I led these locusts over the newly widened and repaved road, which smelled like a burning fuse and which had no painted line yet and which made a wavering vapor of César's and Frank's legs and butts. We passed silent road grading and tar machines. I could not stop walking, I do not know why, could not stop. I moved over the hidden ancient ruts, my hard shoes clacking, shrugging myself down the hill.

Red, the donkey. My shoes clacked, my parts flapped, and my red-and-gray-haired butt and flanks swayed. Around me the air was no more than the breath of an owl, but it stirred the fresh golden straw strewn by the roadbuilders over the hilly aprons of 185. From the highway a dirt road led a little way east to the chewed-up ground of the parking spaces and the hangar.

The old, bony lion at the festival entranceway shook his head when he saw the crowd. He shook his huge, almost hairless head and asked two questions he knew the answers to: "Who are you? Why are you here?"

We did not answer. Who knows if we ever would have. But the child of the question, the shadow child, stepped forward, and she snatched the stamps and ink pads that were the lion's official chile festival equipment.

"*Gracias,*" she said.

Frank and I inked the stamps and we stamped the hands of the children, APPROVED. We officially APPROVED them and César and the others as they marched in under the Hatch Chile Festival banner. How many had there been at first? Eight families, twenty or thirty others. There were fifty-nine people now. Our children ran to the booths and into the hangar where the square dancers stopped dancing when they saw the horde approaching. A storm of hungering had come. In this kind of storm you know you live on a shore, you live only on sand.

The caller called, "Do the right-left through. Centers pass through. Veer to the left. Now circ-u-late." But when he saw us, he lost his place, and said, "Do a—do a—" The musicians played bravely but uncertainly until the caller said, "Do a walking dodge, and boys trade. First couple left and next couple left, and—" but he didn't say "prom-e-nade!" He said, "Holy shit!"

The band leader set his guitar into a stand behind him. He asked, "What is it?" into the microphone. The caller pointed.

The people at the booths stepped back. After all, they were good people. They watched. It is true some salespeople screamed, some shouted—lame shouting, only bleating.

The People bowed their heads and said, "*Perdóname, querido hermano. Perdóname, querida hermana.*" Forgive me, dear brother. Forgive me, dear sister. And they took what they wanted.

At one corn stand a young man pointed a handgun in the air and shot it. We three naked men charged at him, and he dropped the gun at his feet. Frank put the gun into the young man's boiling kettle full of ears. "Amen," I said, praying it would not go off.

César said, "Sit down! We have not finished."

Frank asked the young man, "Who *are* you?"

The young man, in gang colors, the Good Friday colors, black and black and black, sat in the dust. He could not name himself. He tried, but could not. He braced himself with his hands, looked as dizzy as feathers falling out of heaven.

The shouting around us stopped, and more miraculous surrenderings began. The three sisters Úbeda, Faye, Arlene, and Altadena, freely offered the Christmas decorations they sold for the Bell Fund at Christ Is King church. Faye offered their lace-and-sugar bells and snowflakes. No one wanted them. Only a few accepted her offer of the sections of white lambswool that could be placed under Christmas trees. Faye's son was Sheriff Morales. I knew he would be keeping an eye on her booth, and it worried me.

At one booth where Nike and Reebok ripoffs were sold, the tattooed sellers helped the laborers steal the right sizes. They measured feet. They frowned if they did not have the size. They promised to find it.

And this happened all around.

The Hatch Valley Bear cheerleaders handed out free Cokes and Dr. Peppers. The youngest Segundinas at the Segundina's Best booth wrapped foil around smoked turkey legs and handed them out to our swarm. On command of Señora Segundina, all seven children said "*Thank* you" to us in the special way they had been taught to say it to paying customers.

Frank called, "*Hola,* Señor Mack," as we approached Mack's Rack.

Mack, who was blind, waved at Frank, at exactly where Frank was, and said, "Bishop Velasco! Old friend!"

Frank said, "You remember me?"

"I am fallen away," said Mack, "but I have not fallen far."

"Bless you," said Frank.

With strange tenderness, Mack said, "Bless me, Father."

Frank leaned over the plywood counter and touched Mack's closed blind eyes, a kiss upon the man's soul. Mack had been a singer for Los Zopilotes. A bad blind singer—and how often do you see that? Liston Potter, the leader of the band, had finally asked Mack to quit, and he had.

"Red, César," said Frank, "cast your nets here."

So, we looked over Mack's merchandise. Mack said, "The festival's gotten rowdy, you noticed?"

"A riot," I said.

"Yeah," Mack said, as if he could see everything that was going on. He had no real idea, of course.

Frank tried on some sunglasses. "Not those," I said.

Mack said, "He's right. They don't go with your outfit."

Around us the dead returned to life. The noise of the crowd and our swarm was that sound of sand washing over sand. All the goodness in the people of my valley, their buried kindness, was coming out. Strange to see this love rise from its grave to greet the People.

We tried on many sunglasses before Frank settled on some stylish Paco Rabannes, the wraparound kind. Mack offered an Infant Atocha scarf, which Frank tied onto his head, making four big knots and flaps. César and I chose MackMen billcaps with big truck grilles decaled onto the front. He had MackWomen ones too—curved grilles. Mack insisted that we not pay for any of it.

At the Tejo & Sons booth I filched a poster of a woman passionately loving a motorcycle with her legs and body. Her nose was a good nose. I could practice drawing her nose.

Surrenderings. Everywhere. You are saying, No, no, no. I hear you saying this, and how can I blame you?

The American Legionnaires and the Legionnettes had given our smallest children their goods, all their plastic inflatable ball-peen hammers and three-foot plastic baseball bats and crayons big as kindergartners. The children rode them and bounced them off each other and chewed on pieces of funnel cake and sausage-on-a-stick, and when a group of them wandered onto the concrete dance platform, Liston Potter picked up his honey-colored fiddle. His left knee bent, left hip barely started to move, lips pursed up, shoulders peaked, and the music he unwound was the whole bright ribbon of his heart.

The square dancers were men in black shirts, black jeans, boots, and black hats with silver concha hatbands, and women in tiered layers of white and black petticoats and white blouses with ruffled plunging necklines, and silver concha necklaces. They invited the children into the lines. Some men gave the children their hats. Some women gave them necklaces.

What we were not given, we stole. We stole what we needed, and who can ever say how much is enough?

To steal fifty pounds of onions, a man who always eats alone must be dreaming of sizzling butter and cilantro and stolen potatoes and the stolen affections of a hundred hungry guests. A woman who steals the "Sassy Pants" from the Hatch Extension booth, what does she want with them? She doesn't fit into them. She probably doesn't know who would fit, not one person. Impulse stealing. But if she had a daughter, if she had a daughter instead of a son, and if her daughter was not gone, if and if and if, then she would say, "For you, *mi hija*," and give her the jean cutoffs (black, sexy lace sewn on the pockets and legs), and she would say, "They're called Sassy Pants. They're hot!"

What has she stolen? One priceless *If*, marked "$12—Homemade."

"Is that you?" someone asked me. Impossible to mistake her voice.

Recita Holguín.

"Red," she whispered. She was behind me. Frank, César, they disappeared the way men disappear in the Bible miracles.

I moved closer to the Tejo & Sons table. I did not turn around. Buck naked, you know. I gripped my rolled-up motorcycle poster, and said, "Recita, I am naked, my dear."

She said nothing. How much silence is possible in a throng? Only the stars at night know. She stood very close to my back. "You are a beautiful man," she said. "And brave."

What to say? I said, "Go away, Recita."

Poplar leaves fall the way her hands fell then upon my

waist, her smooth wrists sliding over my sides, her cool fingers rustling over, landing on my stomach.

I said, "You are—everyone is—" I unrolled my poster. "Please, Recita," I said, but she stayed. Did I imagine the silence? No talking, no song, and no square-dance calling. I would have given anything to hear one Segundina say one "*Thank* you." I held up the poster to hide me.

When I turned around, I turned inside her hands, her fingers now on my hips.

"Brave," she said, or she said, "Be brave." Her shoulder-length black and silver hair was swept back. As many crooked lines were in her narrow, bony face as in the rings of old trees. Her eyes ignited the skin of my own face.

You can see—can you see?—how terrible this miracle was. Inside me, I prayed, "Jesus Mary Joseph! This—me and Recita—this dream *had* to come true *here*? Now?"

She leaned forward. She gazed down at my parts. "I see you are ready for battle, Red Greet." As simple as raising a window blind, she took away the poster, looked close at the woman loving the motorcycle. "My," she said, and rolled the poster in her hands, rolled very slowly, her hands almost touching each other. I do not know what she did with the poster because next she embraced me, her head at my neck, the smell of her hair like balsamic oil, her warm left ear against my throat, her hands moving down my hips, each finger writing psalms.

The sounds of the festival crowd, noises, splinters of words, returned, and Liston Potter's fiddle, and the locusts, the People, the singing, the laughter and souls waking, the kissing noises on my neck, and Tejo murmuring, "Go fer it, man." I saw the disappearing and reappearing identical red bowler hats of the sisters Úbeda, who were the friends of Recita and who had been the friends of Cecilia.

"What will you do now?" Recita asked. "Do you know? Do you?"

(Have I said that it was her singing that had made me fall in love with her?) "Do you?" she asked again.

I cannot explain how obscene our lusting in the church had been, or how sacred. Sacred and obscene as snare drums and saxophones at High Mass. We were a bad musical, Frank was right.

She whispered, "Do you know what you will do?"

I answered her, "We will go to Eusebio's and to the Bishop's lands. All of us will stay. Permanent." I asked, "Will you come?"

She said yes.

In miracles, no one says no.

Rise and sin no more, Jesus says.

Yes.

If you touch my wounds, will you believe? Jesus asks.

Yes.

Walk upon the water. Serve wine from the empty jars. Give the thousand these five loaves and five fishes.

Yes. Yes. Yes.

She walked with me, she took my hand, and we joined César and Frank under the Hatch Chile Festival banner, the throng returning to us like moths to the horns of the moon. It was late in the day, hot.

The police had come to make arrests. Sheriff Morales asked me, "You have any suggestions about how I'm gonna haul you all away?"

Did one square dancer question him? One Extension person? One onion or chile or fake-Nike seller?

The sheriff looked at Frank. "You are a bishop," he said.

Frank said, "If you say so."

"We will walk to the jail," I said to Sheriff Morales. You

see, I had Recita's hand inside my hand. I held it like a stolen
thing, and wanted not to let it go.

"Long walk," said Sheriff Morales. He did not want us in
his jail, you could see that. He offered his leather jacket to the
Bishop.

The Bishop did not know what to say or do. He accepted
the jacket.

Me? I held Recita's hand. It was all I thought about.

"We will walk," said César, and already he led the way to
the dirt road and south onto the highway. Sheriff Morales followed us in his police car.

We walked where the Río Grande has claimed and
reclaimed the land many times, where the settlers and sellers
and buyers made bankers' and miners' and railroaders' and outlaws' dreams come true. We walked where the farmers and
herders and lawmen fought, and the troops stood guard and the
Mexican and Texan tyrants cashed in and the Church sold out,
and where the unsaved souls of the Conquistadors walked and
still walk and will always. A long way. It is a long way.

If I show the treasure map of our valley, you will say, "I
have seen this." If I show you the mysteries like those on the
tilma of Juan Diego who was blessed with confusion by La
Virgen de Guadalupe, you will say I am simpleminded.

Be simpleminded with me. Draw a cross through our valley, with the center at Las Almas. Put the long beam north to
south, from Hatch to Chamberino. Put the crossbeam east to
west, from the Sierra de la Soledad to the west mesa. If you
have a pirate's heart, here is what you see: crowded together at
the center are the "historic homes" and the "old downtown"
and the barrio and the banks and the porno shop and the law
offices and the police station and courthouse and library. Far
south, past the university, past the farmland and Stahmann
pecan orchards and San Albino cemetery, is where we are

parceling the acreage with new and old money. Far north, in the subdivided farmlands around Eusebio's map dot and past the pecan orchards on the way to Hatch, we have begun plowing with new and newer money. Far west, past motel row and on the way to the municipal airport, new businesses have begun sowing out-of-town money. In the east, past the new Wal-Mart and K-Mart and Montgomery Ward, and past the new mall and the renovated hospital and the doctors' office complexes and the new beehive developments and upscale old and new money, and right up to the foothills of the Sierra de la Soledad we have reaped the newest new money.

Do you see what we saw? You must be simpleminded to see it, I think.

The moon came out, coppery until it could rise above the El Paso pollution that had crossed into New Mexico. Walking south, we could look into the whole valley: the shape of things to come.

The Bishop had wrapped the sheriff's leather jacket around his waist so that, with his floppy Atocha scarf and naked chest and legs, he looked like crazy John the Baptist. When he stopped in the center of the highway, we stopped too. He said we should turn around, walk north to Eusebio's home.

Sheriff Morales's car slowed down. It turned with us and cruised next to us for a while before he parked on the shoulder of the road. He did not roll his window down as we walked past.

We heard him honk a few minutes later. He did not follow.

The moon rose higher, grew smaller. At the edge of Eusebio's brick patio, we built a bonfire. We unlocked all his doors. We crowded into Eusebio's rooms, raided his closet of wine, ran his water, read the words in his books, teased his guard poodles guarding nothing anymore.

César and the Bishop and I went outside to dress behind Eusebio's LeBaron. Recita had unbundled my clothes for me. Shy before the others now, she turned around while I dressed. But then she tucked my shirt in, and whispered, "Red," each time she stabbed her hands down my pants.

Suddenly, Recita said, "There!" and pointed. Inside the LeBaron was a woman, and with the woman was the child wearing the shirt on her head. The child grinned at us, showed us her fist as if to ask us a question about whatever it was she held. Without one moment of hesitation, the Bishop kneeled before her car window. He bowed his head. The woman with the child frowned at the Bishop. The child herself played with the switch for the interior light, and ignored him.

"Who is she?" I asked.

"Damaged," said César. "My sister and I are her caretakers."

"I don't understand," said Recita.

César said, "Mental-damaged. No parents."

What the child held up was a leather garden glove, one garden glove, left hand, and she showed it to us again.

The woman opened the car door. She took the child with her into Eusebio's house. I don't know why we stayed at the car, but we did, and looked inside for the match of the glove, all three of us. César said, "The child's question—'Who you are?' She asks everyone this question. Someone told her she belonged to no one, that no one belonged to her. She thinks she will find her parents. 'Who are you?' she asks. Every adult, she asks it."

When we finished, our fists were full of car trash. I found the match for the glove. I pulled it over my left hand. I said, "I feel like playing baseball."

"Baseball?" asked Recita.

"Good idea!" said the Bishop.

On Eusebio's patio, I untied a long *ristra* of red chiles,

and spilled them out. Recita and César and the Bishop and I batted them from the patio with a crooked mesquite stick. The chiles rattled when the stick broke them. The wind or the land scattered the seeds from the pods. The puffs of stinging powder made us all cough, laugh, choke, cry every time at bat. I hit the farthest, which César said was because I had the best stick, and which Recita said was because I cared the least of all of us about destroying Eusebio's chiles, and which the Bishop said was because of the glove and the home-field advantage.

According to the laws of the Church, which are not the laws of the State, the Bishop was banished to the La Florida Deluxe Apartments in Anthony, New Mexico. His amazement with all people and things, all human and heavenly events, increased and multiplied. As he said, he left the tomb, truly he left it.

As for the People, they crossed the Río Grande into Mexico again. We are all Noah's children, crossing the waters, crossing and waiting at the borders. Time has proven this.

I ask you why we should not welcome the migrant flood. Time has proven it will come. History—the Liar—knows. Everything that is ours will be theirs and ours. After the flood, we will have only as much as we had once: the homesteads claimed and settled, and seeds spilled, and old trees felled and rough timbers raised. The church bells ringing, damming and undamming God inside us. And the holy, terrible spirit of Nature forever making Noahs of us.

For fourteen days at the end of July, Mrs. V served Mr. V the lemonade my mother had brought each evening. Whatever was left over, Mrs. V had to return to us because to throw away holy water was sacrilege.

Each day Mother made the lemonade, she prayed into the pitcher: "Fountain of Heaven, where there is drought bring rain. Mother of God, where there is drowning bring baptizing. Ark of Peace, where emptiness is bring blessing."

Frank was there for the ritual, and so was I. At the mouth of the round pitcher, the liquid trembled as my mother prayed. We saw. We saw how you held the pitcher, gazing into it, Mother. You looked without fear at your own belief reflected back, how shallow it could be, how endlessly deep.

By the end of the first week, Frank and I had memorized the magic words, and we mouthed them into our RC colas at Gamboa's. Fountain of Heaven. Mother of God. Ark of Peace. The whole thing. I prayed the prayer right. I was sincere. Frank was not. "Piece of ark," he said. "Mother of Todd. Fountain of Fords." To his eternal regret, I have remembered his sacrilege and my sincerity. Why have I remembered?

Mrs. V was supposed to say this prayer a certain way into

the glass before she served it to Mr. V. I believe that is what she did. But it is possible she said a different prayer.

How many glasses of holy lemonade did she serve Mr. V? I have wondered. I see her now, her face traced out in the burning air, her prayer mixing blood and water with words. And how many times did Mr. V take one drink of the hyssop and shout at her, his face grinding against her face or his shouting sawing at her neck and the back of her head, the spirit tearing from her like scourged flesh. And another drink from the glass, and his hand probably softly resting on Frank's shoulder, no need to grip, but his fingers digging in the fabric of Frank's shirt, and how many drinks from the glass and her begging him to stop, and then Mr. V holding the pitcher close to her face as if to scrape out her eyes with it, and that bitter smell of crushed lemons and her skin trembling from the words struck hard against it.

Through the walls once, I heard Mrs. V beg for him to stop. Frank and I had taken the lemonade there to his mother. Walking back alone, I decided to steal the empty dog bowl I saw on the back porch of their neighbor, Doña Esther Mérida, mother of Sister María Josefa, the Carmelite nun who had catechized me and Frank and Eusebio and Cecilia and the Úbeda sisters. So many of us.

I wanted that one half of a perfect sphere. New. White.

Her dog, a hound puppy, allowed me to take the bowl, moved its nose up, up, up, as if to say, "New! Pretty! Take it!" I held the bowl with both hands and looked inside, my red face waning and waxing according to how I tilted the shining bowl. On the underside: *Hecho en Mexico.*

I could hear Mrs. V beg. "I am your wife," she said.

"Who?" Mr. V shouted the word. He never struck her with his fist or with an object, though Frank said that when his father was in a fit, the way his hands gripped his belt made them seem like the heads of snakes.

"Who do you think you are? Bitch-fucking-bitch!" Mr. V shouted. "Who are you?"

Why was this question, three words, and only words, so terrifying? A gunpowder prayer, a fire in a flower. The fire ran in all directions, like burning petals and then golden tongues falling out of heaven.

I stood still in Doña Mérida's garden. I saw an apparition. Truly, an apparition. What I saw floating above Doña Mérida's tall larkspur and spindly cosmos entranced me. A freshly painted flamingo, wings half open, body tilted up, neck extended and head and open eyes already in flight.

Out of the furnace came another question. "Why are you here?" It must have been asked of Frank. Was he asking Frank why he should be there in his own father's home? I only half-remember it now, because I was already pulling up the long wire stakes attached to the endless legs of Doña Mérida's flamingo, and cradling the creature, getting white and fluorescent pink paint on my arms.

I brought her and my white bowl to my hiding place. Small well. Small tree. Small house with a thick book for a door. Standard Diary. Great Flamingo watching over all. I upended the white bowl to make a perfect egg under her.

I walked to the Alcedama place to visit my father, who, of course, asked about my pink and white arms.

"Mrs. V is painting a chair," I said, wishing for the sake of the lie that I had paint on the seat of my pants.

He didn't look up from his work. He didn't ask about Mrs. V. He set the last rocks into the ground at the farthest point of the Alcedamas' property. He said, "That boy," and couldn't say more.

Was he talking about Frank? Was he talking about me? About Frank, I think.

During the fourteen days I had delivered the lemonade to the Velascos, my father had almost completed building the

Alcedamas' wall. The low wall curved round all the land that hard work, love, and luck had brought this good family, and made me see now that they owned very little, though it was so much more than we had. The rock pieces—how many?—I was silently counting them—they were like questions of different sizes my father mortared together into one question.

He could see me silently counting the big rocks and the smaller rocks he called spalds. His eyes never wandered from mine. "Beauty," he said. The one word. "Beauty."

You can see, he was looking deeply into me, naming what he saw. Beauty. He was offering an explanation of the Alcedamas' need for the wall. Beauty. He was naming why he needed to build such walls. Beauty. He was trying to understand why I needed to steal the things I had stolen. Was he trying to make me understand too? Were you, Father?

And I see now how he named to himself a larger purpose: that he would overcharge the Alcedamas—charge them twice what was fair—and give all the extra money to the Velascos.

Beauty! Five hundred and sixty dollars.

When Mr. Alcedama and my father met the next week, Mr. Alcedama unfolded the original handwritten estimate. He looked at the outrageous charges, criminal, beautiful. He slowly folded the piece of paper in the careful way you fold something you entrust to a robber. He handed it to my father. "Good," he said. That is all. We knew him all at once, this stranger, this rich man who made stealing from him so easy. Is it any wonder I have been a thief my whole life? I learned early that the desire to lose is as powerful as the will to own and gain. The people who help others lose, they are part of a priesthood.

Mr. Alcedama explained that he would have to pay half then and half on the second Sunday in September. He asked this question: "What have I bought, Mr. Greet?"

My father put the money, cash, in his back left pocket.

Two hundred and eighty dollars. He didn't look at Mr. Alcedama, and Mr. Alcedama didn't ask the question again. He knew my father planned for all of the money, the first and second payments, to be given to Mr. V.

At the wagon, both men patted the head of our old dray. "Blessings," said my father.

Mr. Alcedama said it too. "Blessings, Mr. Greet."

Driving away, we saw him walk along his new wall, a humble necklace that had been a mountain. At home that evening, my mother served us the leftover lemonade Mrs. V had brought. My mother sweetened it for us. She asked, "You have enough?"

Mr. V accepted the money from my father. This good fortune made a change in Mr. V. Who knows? Maybe the lemonade made the difference. On the same weekend that he received the money, Mr. V asked to be forgiven, and truly was by Frank and by the priest in the confessional, and by the parish to whom he witnessed his shame, and by God, and, probably, by Mrs. V.

Miracles. My father moved mountains. My mother saved souls. Should I not believe in miracles?

When I decided to ask Recita Holguín to marry me, I visited my confessor, the Bishop, in his place of banishment.

"Red!" he said. "Red!" And he hugged me close, his cheek and ear pressed hard against my chest. He stepped back, and raised up on his toes, and held his arms over my shoulders to bless me: "Fountain of Heaven. Mother of God. Ark of Peace." This old blessing of strange and disturbing power brought tears to us both. His bony chest contracted against me. My nose ran. I had no handkerchief and had to use my hand. I snicked the stickiness from one side of my nose, then the other, onto the La Florida Deluxe parking lot.

"God bless you," he said as if I had sneezed. His one-room apartment had a hide-a-bed sofa, long, wide, but with thin cushions. He said, "It is the place to sit."

I said, "Nice," rested my butt and hands on the dull green and vermilion mysteries in the fabric.

The band of freckles across his dark nose and cheeks made his face a galaxy of amazement, made his large eyes seem larger and his wide forehead wider. No end to the horizons of his joy. I had admired these freckles when we met for the first time as children in 1915; I had seen them for eighty-one years of friendship, and in memory the afterimage of them has not faded. When he sat down near me, he said, "I have planned! I have imagined your visit, Red. You are a dream!"

He rested his hands inside mine. Yes, I held them. Holding them gave me such pleasure I should be ashamed to confess it. But I am less afraid than I once was of allowing that there is a kind of touching friends do that should be called lovemaking. Ask old women friends, old men friends, old married couples, ask them if I am right.

How dear the Bishop's hands were to me! And how different. They, too, were now covered with freckles. I said, "What are these?"

"Nasturtiums," he said, thinking I had asked about the overlapping vermilion and green faces in his sofa. Perenially, flowers blossomed in his thoughts.

I asked again, "*These?*" His fingers were freckled, and his palms. "They're everywhere!"

His wrists and arms were freckled. His neck. He bowed his head to show me his freckled scalp. He said, "God is Lord of Tattooists, no?"

"Sure is," I said. Amazed. Upset.

I strained not to imagine the number of freckles. But I am a counter, I don't know why. All my life I have felt the need. I counted rocks in the rock walls my father built for a living; the number of people who received communion at Sunday Mass; the hats on the heads in Albertson's Superstore; the trees in the Christmas tree lots. I counted money in my dreams before I ever stole it, counted it as I stole it (put back anything over the planned amount), counted it after I stole it. Money, trees, hats, holy people, rocks. Whatever was beautiful to me I wanted to know the amount of its beauty. The Bishop's freckles. Numberless.

"I have a fire over me," the Bishop said. They did look like tiny rising or collapsing flames. "What dark angels hover over you, Red?"

"My problems are nothing," I said. "My sins are crumbs."

"Impossible!" he said. "Your sins have always been loaves! I have feasted on your sins, Red!"

I wanted to please him. How could I not want that? I said, "I have kept secrets. From Recita."

"You have. You have? Of course you have!" He tugged at my hands to lift me from the sofa. "Don't start your confession yet. We'll eat first. Eggs. Wine. Cottage cheese. Everything is already prepared."

He sliced hard-boiled eggs with the egg slicer I had given him. He served full glasses of wine, one of the twelve bottles I had lifted for him from Eusebio's cellar. The cottage cheese was small curd. We sprinkled red chile pepper over the egg slices (ten for me, twelve for him) and into the cheese.

I said, "I will be direct. I'm going to ask Recita to marry me."

"Wonderful," he said.

"Wonderful," I said. "It is. Wonderful. But I worry." The golden yolk on my tongue crumbled. I didn't know what to say next.

"Tell what you can, Red."

"After so many years. There are questions."

"On earth as in heaven, Red." He coughed. "What is the big question—*la pregunta grande?*"

"Impotency," I said. "Will I be impotent?"

"*Dios!*" He coughed hard. He wiped bits of shiny egg from his lips. "I think—I think we should finish our meal," he said.

"I don't know. I might be unready. Alone twenty-three years."

The chili powder, too much chili powder, made him gasp. He said, "You are old, my friend. But she is also." He sprinkled more powder on his egg slice, both sides. "The dust settles. It can be kicked up again." His lips were red as a harlot's.

"Sins are involved," I said. "Impure thoughts. Things I have not told her."

"Oh. Oh!" What food before him could satisfy him like this news? He said, "The coffee is already made. Fresh ground. Smell it?" He wiped his hands with his napkin, but not his mouth. "So. We will go to the confessional sofa. You will tell me."

I told him about La Memoria.

You have heard of the tradition of setting the table for a dead loved one? People will do this in order to pretend. They will invite the Memory back. They will put the chair and setting where La Memoria sits. They will serve the soup and bread that are La Memoria's favorites. How many ice cubes does La Memoria like in the glass? What brand of creamed corn gave so much simple pleasure? This is how the ritual of the meal with the dead goes. For a while after the person dies we set a place for and serve a meal to La Memoria. We invite others among the living to come. Then, we do this on the family birthdays, the name-saint day, the anniversary of marriage, the holidays, the anniversary of death. We invite others among the dead to come. The ritual is crowded with memories. The table is laden with good food. It gets expensive. Eventually, we invite La Memoria less often to the table. We celebrate alone. Once a year maybe.

We pretend. We imagine the departed one, La Memoria, is clever at the table, clever and kind, and a generous listener and always interested and utterly infatuated and in love with us and transformed by our love, the ways that, truly, the departed one was. Except better. We pretend everything was better.

Or we imagine the departed one was swilling food and drink like a sow, and grunting and cruelly ignoring our cleverness, our kindness and generosity, our perfect love that La Memoria is and always was undeserving of. La Memoria makes us do the dishes, clean the table, sweep the floors. La Memoria leaves us to go watch the television. Good riddance to this memory. "Praise God," we say until the next meal for the dead.

When Cecilia died in 1972, I honored her. La Memoria. Alone in our bedroom, I made our bed, small queen-sized caved-in bed, as she liked it. I washed the lace flounce, a lace of falling-rain pattern, and I ironed it, and said, "Cecilia. How much?" I sprayed as much starch as she liked and I ironed out every wrinkle. I put on the old bed pad she had always said was good enough, and I heard my dead wife, La Memoria, say that it was, it was "Good enough, dear Red."

With my hands and with the insides of my arms, I made the white sheets smooth. I put on Cecilia's quilt, the prized quilt. Her mother had bought it for her in Tijuana from someone who said it was an American Civil War quilt traded across the border and traded back, and worth fortunes. Across her quilt flew lariats of morning glory vines, and inside the lariats flew stars the same pale blue color as the flowers. When everything was made right, I closed the curtains of our room.

Well. You can imagine. A man alone. I pretended. And each time I pretended, La Memoria became a more remarkable lover, and La Memoria's lover, Red Greet, became a lover's dream.

I lay longer with La Memoria. I lay every afternoon, in the late afternoon, with La Memoria. Already, I was in love with Recita—in celibate but passionate love. I should have separated from my dead wife. Death should have helped me. But La Memoria and I would not give up this time together, which was like no time we had ever known in the living years.

One day, I stripped off the quilt. I piled all our old wraps and cloaks and coats and jackets on top of the bed. We seemed to be hosting a party, La Memoria and I. So many people had come, the dead and living, and I imagined them as gracious guests, excited by each other's company, sharing the dip and heaven and earth's gossip, pouring each other wine from bottles that never emptied, linking arms and hands and spilling everywhere, singing badly and angelically, burying old miseries and raising up old joys.

Through the door, one guest said, "Cecilia, you should be ashamed of yourself. You are dead!"

La Memoria groaned, "How can I be sure?"

Another guest said, "Red! This is sad. This is not good."

"How can I be sure?" I said.

Our guest said good-bye from behind the door, and we said good-bye back. "Good-bye," we said to them. "Good-bye! Blessings! Good-bye!" and said it to each other, and we closed the spaces between us. Tightly. And La Memoria and I remembered she was dead, but the sadness sharpened our pleasure. In my bliss, I flung off the wraps and jackets, coats and cloaks. The last of our guests left. ("It is not sad," the guest whispered through the door. "It is beautiful." Her voice was Sister Josefa's.)

The front door closed with a sound like a last breath. I flung off more coverings. The bed was bare. I was alone. I moved my hands and the insides of my arms over the bed and could barely believe La Memoria had gone.

What more do I need to confess?

I still make the bed so many ways. Year after year. I hardly recognize the bed. And who is this La Memoria who visits: a thousand different Cecilias, and none of them really Cecilia. Who is this man who almost every afternoon for twenty-three years has been pretending? How will I ask Recita, dear Recita, a living woman, to lie with me? I will disappoint her. I will disappoint me.

"Complicated," the Bishop said. "Weird. And complicated. And familiar." He leaned toward me on the confessional sofa.

His freckles were tiny *tilmas*. "I am celibate. I know this story. If this is a confession, I do not know absolution that will fit."

"Huh?" I said.

He said, "I have old beer in the refrigerator. Bring it."

"No absolution?" I said. I went to the refrigerator.

Dos Equis. Four of them. I put them on the counter and wrestled with the tops. "They're not screwtops," I said. "Do you have an opener?"

"Bring them, Red."

He unscrewed them, of course. He was an angel, the Bishop. He wiped the moist bottom of the bottle across the fabric of the sofa. He swigged. "You need a plan," he said.

"Right!" I said. "That's what I need."

The Bishop had no plan. "You must pray for a plan," he said.

"Damn!" I said. "You have to do better than that."

He swished his beer in his mouth. The freckles over his skin were filled with dark red roses no larger than motes. "It is what I do," he said. "I pray. I pray to the saints and holy martyrs for a plan."

I asked, "Which ones do you pray to?"

"The women. Saint Joan. Teresa of Ávila. Saint Bridget, Saint Monica."

"The real lookers," I said.

He hummed. His hum meant yes.

"And? And you have a plan?"

"I have no plan," he said.

"Sixty years! Sixty years of praying, and you have no plan!" I stood up. "This is not encouraging," I said.

What could he say? He said nothing. Finally, he asked me to sit back down. "I love you, Red," he said. "You know this?"

"I know," I said.

"You love me?"

"I love you."

"Red! That is a miracle, is it not? A miracle!"

We had some flan. The flan and the beer did not go well together, but it inspired him. The nutmeg on the flan upset his stomach, and the indigestion inspired him. "Here is my advice," he said. "Do not pray alone. When you are with Recita and La Memoria, when the three of you are together, pray then."

In the motel parking lot, he asked as a favor that I take his Monte Carlo, that I be its caretaker. In the trunk, clothed in the Bishop's vestments and cinched with his gold rope sashes, was his father's mariachi guitar.

In church at the evening service, I whispered "Marry me" to Recita. We were standing close, too close, singing. I made sure she heard. Into her good ear I whispered, "Marry me." This was at the time of the processional song, so that she would have the liturgy, Eucharist, and final blessing during which to consider.

When we left the church, wind freed wisps of Recita's black, red, and silver hair around her dark face. She lifted her head and neck to let wind expose her however it wished. The blue-brown slackness under her eyes was dear to me. And the sharp brightness at her cheeks where the bones grew dull beneath the skin. Her jaw and chin looked small when she gritted her teeth, closed her mouth in a tight smile that showed fear but showed no shame.

My nose watered. I had to wipe it and my eyes too. I am a broken, leaking donkey. She saw this, and lent me a Kleenex from her purse, white alligator-skin vinyl. She handed me the whole purse so I could take another. Never had she done this, though my nose always watered in the cold and watered when I ate and watered when I laughed good, and so I had often asked her for Kleenexes.

She *had* decided to marry me.

117

I knew for sure because she let me hold her hand on the steps of the church. At the bottom steps she closed her long, wrinkled fingers over mine, and pressed our bony fingers, five flinty petals holding up another five, to her breast. She held that flower of old bones to her breast, and bowed her head and smelled the flower. Or it seemed like she smelled it, the way she drew in her breath, so far inside.

In my other hand I held her purse, small, almost empty. Through the vinyl skin I felt coins, two lipsticks, no, three, and a balled-up scarf and a fork and knife, a spoon. Soup spoon.

This was March 31, 1995, the Feast of Eucharist and the Holy Orders. A frost sometimes comes in late March to our valley, a murdering frost. It is carried in the winds that have been waiting in the Sierra de la Soledad, waiting until they can come down to claim all the green, hopeful souls of plum and peach and apple trees.

"What do you plan for us?" Recita asked.

"Plan?" I said. "I am *eighty-six*. You are *eighty-five*."

"You have no plan?" She, of course, did. Instantly, I saw she did, that during the Mass she had made a Plan. I wondered if she had made her own visit to the Bishop's apartment.

Our hands fell apart. We walked beside each other in the night. No words. Had she said yes to my marriage proposal? Now I was not sure. Would she tell me her Plan? Was part of her Plan to keep the Plan secret? Already, maybe we were following her Plan.

An old woman with a Plan—nothing can save you from this. I tell you, if Christ in the desert had met an Old Woman with a Plan and Two Lipsticks and a Soup Spoon instead of meeting only Satan, His suffering, death, and resurrection, all of it, would have begun that very moment, with no man in sight. No apostles, no Judas, no high priests, no soldiers, no Barrabas, no Pilate, no heaven-bound thief on His right side, no hell-bound thief on His left. And no words.

No words. None. On the corner of Mr. Telles's front yard, we passed a shivering old Santa Rosa plum tree, all its fruit doomed. I thought of La Memoria. How strange I must have looked: Recita on one arm, La Memoria on the other.

Finally, I asked, "*You* have a plan?" For the first time, I realized we were not walking to her apartment on Espina and Boutz, where I would usually be allowed one kiss, one embrace, a long one sometimes but only one. I asked, "Where are we going?" We were not holding hands, but she was leading, I was following. "Where?" I asked.

She did not answer. We walked, Recita and I. And La Memoria. Recita's old legs were tough as the roots of sarsaparilla, and lovely all the way up. I could imagine. I did imagine. Too much I imagined.

Inviting legs, but no words.

I am a dishonest man, everyone knows this about me. But I am a little honest whenever I tell a story, and I do not put words where there are no words.

We came to the Bishop's house, which had once been Frank's house when he was still bishop. She said, "We will go into his garden. He has a greeeen house." She did not say "greenhouse," she said, "greeeen house," a very sly way she said this, a sixteen-year-old girl's smile on her face. We opened the gate at the back of the Bishop's garden, Recita pushing it open, La Memoria pushing it closed behind us, do you see? Her Plan.

It was true. The small house was greeeen. The door was a brighter yellow-green, the doorknob was emerald-green glass. Its good coolness made my hand ache, my palm burn. I said, "Doesn't open."

"No?" She opened it without a sound. This made her giggle. "Like I dreamed," she said. She had a dime-sized coffee-spill birthmark on her thick, wide nose, right in the center. It had fingerprint whorls in it. I liked this mark, an uneven oval, which she said was twin to such a mark on her mother and all her mother's ancestors.

Moonlight splashed silver upon the windows that had been painted green. On the wooden floor everywhere were shriveled, sharp-smelling bulbs we scooted our feet through. "Irises," she said. The warped tables along the walls were bare and their speckled Formica had been washed clean, so clean the black-green light on them was like one current of river flowing over another darker current.

"Tell me," she whispered. She was behind me, close enough I could feel her long dress sweep the back of my ankles. Her nose brushed against my ear, and she kissed the tender place behind it and then before it, and whispered, "Tell me," and she kissed the place beneath my ear, old, wrinkled, smelly, hairy ear. Ear of a donkey. I was supposed to tell her. Tell her what? Tell her my Plan, which I didn't have.

"Are you there?" I asked. You can see, I was asking La Memoria, who was once Cecilia herself, if she was still there with us. I didn't feel her at my side.

Recita said, "She is gone."

"She is, isn't she?" I said.

When I dropped Recita's purse on the floor, the things inside it clinked.

She turned me around to face her, and in the turning she slipped off her shoes. Pale yellow, to match her straw-gold dress. Long sleeves, gold trim at the neck and wrists and hem. Tiny gold cloth buttons down the front. She was as tall as me without her shoes.

The purse slumped, and it clinked. Alone, untouched, it made a racket. Recita pushed away the purse with her bare feet. She took my hands, both at the same time, and tugged at them until they understood where they should go. My fingers slid into my back pants pocket where she sent them. She kissed a burning path across my jaw, nudged my chin with her chin. She tucked in my thumbs too.

Her cheek pressed against mine. With her own hands she touched her face, her jaw and chin, her fingers blessing her own eyebrows and eyelids. She closed her eyes to touch her ears, old and worn, but worn smooth by time or by the caressing of her own fingers over time. "Red. Tell me. You have a plan?"

I swear, the bulbs strewn over the floor gathered around my ankles, gathered and grew fingers. I kicked them away. They crept back.

At the same moment my hands tried escaping, her arms captured my waist: her hands flew into my back pockets. She said to me, said to my hands, "Stay inside." Her fingers between my fingers, she pushed my hands flat against my hips. She wanted my hands to go deeper into my pockets and so she forced them down, gentle but sure, which brought my pants low on my hips. "Stay there," she said, and her fingertips showed my fingertips the curve of my own flesh, inviting me to touch. Touch myself.

"Recita," I said. "My dear."

She said, "You are shy."

I said, "This place is muggy."

"Ohhh, Red," she whispered, "we are in a greeeen house." Her hands withdrew, her moist palms dampening my wrists. I watched her hands move behind her. How they moved was mysterious, reaching down behind her. Her lips tried to kiss my eyes closed, but I watched her hands. You would not?

She turned her back to me and bent her knees and waist in order to lift the golden hem of her straw-colored dress, the whole hem. And now I saw how the moonlit green light of the greenhouse made her golden dress the green-gold of cotton blossoms. The smooth material still in her hands, she drew her fingers up against the skin of her ankles and legs, and, slowly, her thighs.

Oh, my dear.

Old woman's underwear. You will not see this underwear in magazines. No designer names, no printed words, no lace or floral wonders, but puckered elastic, plain faded pink cloth, enough to cover a chair.

I have my theories. When this underwear goes on it does not take itself too seriously. When this underwear comes off (Recita's thumbs hooking the waistband, her hands almost completely inside, pushing this underwear down over her knees and ankles), when this underwear comes off (one dance step and she has kicked it away, and it lands around the purse, the silent purse). When this underwear comes off, it is part of a Plan.

Facing me again, she dropped the hem all at once. She did not take off the dress, under which she now had nothing but her legs, lovelier than they had ever been in my imagination.

She touched but did not unbutton the cloth buttons at her breast and neck. How nice they must have felt, the material rougher than the material of her dress. I saw her pleasure. Under her eyes and at her cheeks was lovely greenness gilded by the deep brown of her skin. I became aware of my fingertips enjoying my own flesh.

"Where is your purse?" I asked. I looked around for it. Why did I look for it? Concerned for her purse!

She asked, "Worried?"

"Where has it gone?" I noticed dried white paint drips on the wooden floor of the greenhouse.

"Not far," she said. "She never goes far." She made a little clap of her hands. "Heeeere, purse. Heeeere, purse."

"Lost," I said. My nose trickled.

"Wipe your nose," she said, tender, funny, loving three words, good as any I have ever heard. She leaned her body against me; she reached behind me to free my hands.

I wiped, sniffed, and blew my nose right in front of her, and this seemed not at all strange. She took the rag from me and balled it up and put it back in my pocket for me. What do the young know of this kind of love?

I touched the buttons of her dress, the cloth still heated from her touch. She unbuckled my belt. Buckled it one notch tighter.

We kissed. Our eyes were open. I leaned back from her and looked close at her hair, the falling waves on the top, the retreating flatter waves on the sides, the unbrushed tumble in back.

We kissed. I touched her woman's beard, barely there, but there enough to illuminate the moonsilver on the skin of her neck and jaw. And around her mouth. Silver and seedling green. I tried to pray. This would be the time I should pray. Where was La Memoria? Where had La Memoria gone?

We kissed. Recita's ears were low on her head. Smooth, small ears, low and far back on her head. I prayed: What now, God? When I touched her ears, I swear this, I felt them move back under my fingertips. They *moved*. What plan, God? I need a plan.

We kissed. I had a crazy notion I could move her ears, and if I moved them far enough they would be small wings at the back of her neck. She would fly a little ahead of me with them. Like a golden bee, she would hover over me. I pushed her ears back with my thumbs. She cupped my ears with her hands. My donkey ears.

How our ears delighted us! We laughed together. We kissed. In the greeeen house. It would not be right to tell more about our kiss.

In September Mr. Alcedama paid my father the balance owed. When Mr. V secretly accepted the rest of the money from my father, he began work on a new adobe house for his family. Frank worked near him, worked hard as a man. Mr. V seemed tender toward the boy. He had always seemed that way unless you knew the real truth.

My father sold another little mountain to the Escalantes, close friends to the Alcedamas and co-conspirators in many acts of charity in our valley. Since they were secretive in their good works, we never knew about their charity except through rumor, and how could we believe the rumors, any of us? They were rich. Our natural jealousy of them would have made it easier for them to pass through the eye of a needle than to enter our eyes unbroken.

When the Escalantes paid up, my father bought the radio battery. He sanded and stained and varnished and glued together the cathedral-shaped Atwater-Kent, a wood-carved rose window in it. How a radio should be. With my mother's encouragement, he and I brought the Atwater-Kent to the Velascos.

At the door, Mr. V asked, "What is this?" At once, he realized he had repeated his meanness from our first visit, and he was ashamed, but my father left him room for an act of contrition by grinning and saying, "Gifts, dammit!" Both men laughed.

Mr. V asked us to come inside the half-finished rooms. He had chiseled *nichos* into the walls. He had not gotten *santos* but he would have them, he said. His wife wanted them, and she would have them. "We will have saints and angels in our home again."

The adobe house smelled moist. I could imagine vegetables and flowers growing from the walls. I lifted a soup spoon from the kitchen and I practiced magic. Before their very eyes I put it in my front pants pocket. They did not see. I thought of where the spoon would go. I imagined it inside my small house, at the bottom of my well. I would rub it clean, I would make it shine.

The two men talked about how to install the radio, where it should go, how much of the world the instrument might bring in—on waves. Such marvel then in the word: waves. Our waves, the ones my father and mother saved so long for, would be their waves. Mr. V held up the big Henley radio books, two volumes. He hugged one to either side of his chest like gates he had opened.

At home, my mother asked us how Frank was, how Mrs. V was. We hadn't seen them, we said, and told about the new house, the *nichos*, how clearly you could hear the sound. "Hard to leave," my father said.

To taste a plum you must bite into it. You search its flesh with your tongue. Your mouth softens the fruit and is softened by it. A new kind of hungering comes.

I will not tell about the six months after our kiss. I will not tell about our kiss.

I will tell about our wedding, which was supposed to take place at Christ Is King church, but happened on the Valley View Elementary baseball field on Sunday, September 11, 1995. Why should I not tell about our wedding day?

Hot. A hot day. At Recita's place, making ourselves lunch omelettes with garlic chunks and fresh-roasted chiles, we licked each other's fingers, which made our eyes and lips sting.

I said, "You taste dangerous."

"I am," she said, and because we were sitting at her table in our underwear, I saw the truth of it. A blush spread over her chest. You could make a wish on all that heat, I thought, but didn't know what I could possibly wish, except to take her hand. It blushed, too, at my touch. We seemed to blaze before each other like torches in caves. Oh, I laughed at me—blazing torches and blushes!—Mercy on me!—and she laughed kindly at me. Whenever anyone laughs at me, kindly or unkindly, it makes me feel laughable and, this is the truth: what makes me feel laughable makes me feel innocent. I grew more innocent by the hour in her company.

A little before one o'clock, when the heat was above ninety and climbing, troops of rainclouds came from the south, their shadows darkening the whole valley, darkening it, and raising great walls of dust and blowing them down, and blasting the tops of the trees so they spit the birds from their branches to the ground. "Recita," I said, "this is not good." But when she asked, "Are you frightened?" I did not say yes.

We walked into her small backyard and watched. One faraway, soft clap. One fence-rattling, crashing sound. Two-hundred-foot cartwheels of rain groaned straight north across Las Almas. Not falling rain, but rolling and looping, the way wild mustangs dance and sprint all at once. We were soaked, and had no good reason to go inside.

The storm moved on. The sun came behind it, bending one rainbow over the mountains and bending one around, entirely around them.

If you included my father, whose ghost seemed to have come with the storm, nine people were there waiting for us at Valley View Elementary. At two o'clock when the wedding should have started, we found the doors of the church locked. We had been told they would be. Our banns had been announced each Sunday since August the twenty-first. But official letters from the Diocesan Tribunal to us and to the Bishop said that a ceremony performed by the Bishop would be "unauthorized."

The Bishop's keys did not fit the three locks on each of the ten-foot double doors.

"I am not authorized!" said the Bishop, newly amazed by the insult, and amazed that Recita would kick the doors so hard and so many times with her white wedding shoes. "I am not authorized!" he roared, a sparrow roaring like a lion. He wore no vestments. His black shoes were shabby and his white shirt unlaundered. "Open up!" he said.

We stood at the tall locked doors, the Bishop and Recita and I and our wedding guests, including Cleophas Galván, a jailer, a bad dancer, an impatient listener, but a good man. The Bishop kept us there by his will. He was waiting for a miracle, do you see? He closed his fist tight around the keys.

"Kick it again," he said to Recita. She thumped the door with one foot and whispered, "Jesus Mary Joseph," and thumped it with the other. She angrily wiped away tears and the sweat on her face and neck. September in Las Almas is scalding hot.

My nose watered. I could not stop it. Old plumbing.

If my father was alive, he would kick harder and better than any of us. That is what I thought. He would push his hands through his rock-gritty greasy hair, and curse and break the biggest window in the cathedral and then refuse to set foot in the church ever again. I could feel his presence.

Recita's friends the Úbeda sisters, Arlene, Faye, and Altadena, were there, but they would not kick until the Bishop commanded them to. Altadena and Faye kicked politely. Arlene kicked like Lucifer wanting out of heaven. Eusebio joined in. He winced when he kicked. We were kicking an empty building. The priest, janitors, Altar Society ladies, everyone was off duty. God would have to answer the door.

"This is foolish," I said. "We could hurt ourselves."

We sat down on the church steps. Eusebio had brought bottles of champagne in a large wicker basket that also held a jug of holy water and the wedding rings. He opened two bottles, which we passed around. It was a little after three in the afternoon. Light lifted up the crown of acacia thorns carved on the church doors, but it was not the glistening light of morning. In the desert the morning shadows bow down, and in the afternoon they fall so sharply they make the yuccas, grass, bushes, everything, rise up from the desert.

The Bishop chugged champagne, said nothing. He hummed. He hummed. He had stopped waiting for a miracle. He was waiting for a sign. He rummaged in the wicker basket. "Praise God!" he said. More bottles.

The steps of the church are steep. Who would notice how steep without good champagne? The Bishop sat on the lowest steps next to Cleophas Galván, close next to him. The shadows falling from Cleophas's nose and brow were exactly the Bishop's. I had never looked so close at this man, twenty years younger than all of us, yet one of us somehow. It is easy to imagine things in that sharply falling light and that heat on a wrecked wedding day in September in Las Almas with your feet throbbing and the champagne scraping the dry plates in your head with a dull knife. I thought I saw in Cleophas's face a certain winged pattern of freckles. Did I recognize his narrow chest and smooth throat and his jawline, that womanly jawline of the Chamuscados?

The Bishop looked through a nearly empty bottle at him and at all of us and at his parked Monte Carlo. On the car hood the airbrushed cathedral window floated like a mirage of blessed and broken sunlight. "Holy shit!" he said—for my sake. Only he and I remembered the caller at the chile festival saying this.

No sign came. Arlene led us in the Hail Mary, and when she said, "now and at the hour of our," she stood and kicked the door instead of saying "death" and kicked it instead of saying "Amen."

"We should cross over," I said, and led the group down the steep church steps. A plan. You can see that I had a plan. This is my problem, that I can make the first part of a plan but cannot plan all the other parts.

Arlene took the Bishop's hand to guide him across the

street to the Valley View playground. There was no shade. Hot summer wind blew across the dirt infield. In May the school had planted a windbreak around the whole playground. Two rows of green afghan pines. The seedling harps sang when the hot currents of air moved through their infant limbs. Greeeen limbs. At the home plate backstop, I said, "Here's good," and everyone agreed.

"There is no shade," said Recita.

"There will be in ten or twelve years," said Cleophas, an intelligent man, a man who could do better than be a jailer.

"Amen!" said the Bishop, pleased always with marvels of foolishness.

Cleophas, the Bishop's guardian angel, wore a new rose-pink shirt and silvery white tie, and a royal purple fringed sombrero wider than his shoulders, and boots, good boots, that jingled. Mexican spurs. In Cleophas's belt holster was a Colt and in his right hand one of those Albertson's-brand disposable cameras. Panoramic. He was almost sixty-five, I guessed, and almost handsome in profile, and when I looked right through his eyes I could see the tenderness and amazed spirit of other eyes I have known. He asked, "May I shoot you, Señor Red?" He wore the gun (like Manuel Hernández Galván's gun), you know. I could not help laughing. I said, "Shoot me right after I take my vows."

He said, "Oh. Oh! That. I meant—I have no bullets anyway." He laughed too. He patted the Colt. "The Bishop asked me to wear it."

"Shoot away," I said.

Arlene said, "Dear God, it is hot," and did not say this to herself or to us but to God. Everyone stood near where Recita and I and the Bishop stood. Home plate.

The Bishop, plenty mad at God, repeated, "Dear God, it is hot," and said, "You will forgive us if this wedding does not go nine innings."

He joined our right hands. His own hands were covered in dark freckles, golden scales. "Repeat," he said: "I, Red Greet, take thee, Recita Holguín, for my lawful wife, to have and to hold, from this day forward, for better, for worse, for richer, for poorer, in sickness and in health, until death do us part."

After Recita repeated her vows, he said, "I join you together in marriage, in the name of the Father, and of the Son, and of the Holy Ghost. Amen." He placed a white silk cord around both our shoulders. The same cord, an heirloom, had rested once on my mother and father's shoulders and on mine and Cecilia's. Eusebio handed Cleophas the uncorked clay jug of holy water, and he handed it to the Bishop, who asked Eusebio to bring out the three rings, two for the bride, one for the groom. He sprinkled them with the water. He sprinkled us. "More?" he asked Recita.

"Please," she said, and he poured water into his small palms and sprinkled more on her face to soothe and cool her.

The Úbeda sisters presented the *arras* to me, the thirteen pieces of silver money which I let slide through my fingers into Recita's. Usually this wedding money was left in the church, but since the doors of the church were closed, Recita handed the thirteen pieces to Altadena.

Recita wore her gold dress with the seven gold cloth buttons and the long pleated skirt. She had not rubbed rouge into her dark face or powdered her birthmark on her nose. Her skin shone with sweat and blushed from the moist heat, and her black eyebrows shone too. Her hair, which she had pulled back with a white scarf, was damp. When I had kissed her in the greeeen house, my fingers had climbed the buttons to her cool throat, where my hands could feel when she swallowed and breathed and could tell when her blood leaped. I had reached for her breasts, but she wanted my hands to stay on her throat where I could know how my kisses commanded her blood and breath and hunger. She wanted to teach me how to kiss. I did not know. Really kiss, I mean. I did not know. Cecilia had not taught me. How did Recita know this? She knew.

The Bishop sprinkled me more because, you see, he saw that I was burning, burning up. He said, "*Adjutorium nostrum in nomine Domini.*"

Cleophas, his favorite server at Mass, said, "*Qui fecit caelum et terram.*"

I remembered. *Our help is in the name of the Lord. Who hath made heaven and earth.*

I remembered how I had brought Cecilia to my secret childhood altar after our wedding ceremony. I had shown her what was left: Pretend well. Pretend house. The small cedar had grown twenty feet. The great bird and giant Standard Diary book were gone.

Cecilia bowed her head. She pulled the narrow bright blue wooden tiara from her hair. Twelve hand-carved stars. She seemed to count them, or to notice that I was counting and to count with me. She said, "If I . . ."

I did not ask her to say more because I knew she wished to talk about Frank. She said, "If I say nothing, I will sin, dear Red."

I said, "Say nothing," and was answered with a whimper.

"Nothing," I warned. Her wedding dress was white with a pale icing of cream-colored lace at her neck and wrists. She lifted it and kneeled on her bare knees at the base of the tree, and I kneeled near her to hear what she would say whether or not I wished her to say it.

She whispered, "Frank showed me this place."

"Say nothing. Cecilia. Please." Impossible, I thought. Never! Why? Never.

"I hoped you would not bring me here," she said. When she rose, something, some kind of imperfect mirror, appeared where her knees had been.

I howled, "Look!" and touched the bottom of the white plastic dog bowl. "The egg!" I said, and started to explain: "There was a—"

"—bird," she said. "A flamingo. And her egg."

"Bless, O Lord, this ring, which we bless in Thy name," the Bishop said in Latin. I guess he could not recall the rest of it. He said, "The rings, Cleophas." Eusebio held them out to Cleophas in his open palms, his soft, manicured hands. Again, the Bishop sprinkled holy water on the rings and on me. Only me this time. "Repeat," he said: "With this ring, I thee wed, and I plight unto thee my troth."

Recita vowed it too. The Bishop made the sign of the cross. He recited, "Confirm, O God, that which Thou has wrought in us."

"From Thy holy temple which is in Jerusalem," Cleophas read from his Manual of Prayers.

"Lord have mercy," said the Bishop.

"Christ have mercy," said Cleophas.

"Lord have mercy." The Bishop said, "Okay!"

I kissed the bride. Her face and mine were damp from the sprinkled water. How fearlessly Recita kisses! I taste her lips. She lets me taste. Her lips teach me when I may taste more: her teeth, but only the sharp edges; her tongue, but only the warm tip.

We kissed too long. Nervous applause from the Úbeda sisters made us stop, but we started again. The Bishop tugged on the white cord around our shoulders. He said, "Amen!" but we did not stop. The Bishop said, "Steeee-rike!"

Cleophas took our picture. Panoramic. We kissed still.

The Bishop said, "Steeee-rike two!"

Eusebio said, "Huh?"

We should have stopped. Altadena jingled the silver pieces in her hands. Faye said, "Recita!" Arlene mumbled, "I don't too feel good much," and her sisters stumbled away after her. The heat.

"Steee-rike three!"

We stopped. My mouth burned like an Easter candle. "Mercy!" I said.

Eusebio said, "Huh?"

The Bishop asked Eusebio, "Is your hearing aid in?" and looked and saw that it was in and said, "Good!" real loud. "Come over here." He put his arm around Eusebio's shoulder and walked him out to the dirt pitcher's mound, where he touched Eusebio's ear, drew out the pink hearing aid, and held it out in front of him. He looked at it the way once my father had looked into a pitcher of lemonade and had asked, "What're you up to?"

At my little altar, sixty-one years ago, on my wedding day, Cecilia tried to explain to me about why Frank had brought her to see my secret place, which he had sworn to me he would show to no one.

She said, "Why did he bring me here?" She wiped tears from her eyes back against her cheeks and made her hair at her temples damp and shining. "You see why, don't you, Red? He wants me to love you more than I love him."

What she did not say was that Frank had brought her there to convince her he could be cruel enough to break a promise to a friend. He wanted to show her she should love him less. And maybe he wanted to tell her that. But he did not.

Cecilia and I spoke of that day. For thirty-eight years of marriage, Cecilia and I spoke of it in order not to be afraid of it.

Cecilia died only a few months before Frank became bishop. A week or two before she died, she asked me if I thought I knew the reasons he had become a priest.

She said, "No. You do not. Only God knows."

After she had become ill she would never allow me to

hold her. I could sit in a chair at her bed, I could bathe her and perfume her hair, but then she asked me to sit at the foot and not at her side.

"Only God knows," I said. "You are right. But we—you and I—we know why he was such a goddamn great priest, don't we?" Losing Cecilia to me had made him great. That was what I thought.

She laughed. By then, her laughter, even that, seemed to come from a shallow cave of bones.

Eusebio stood bowed over, with tears in his eyes, though the Bishop had been gentle removing the hearing device. The Bishop spit on the hearing aid. He polished it against his dirty white shirt. He held it up to the sun to study the volume dial, which he groaned at, and which he adjusted with his fingertips. "Be opened!" he said.

Eusebio said, "Give me that back."

The Bishop placed it in Eusebio's ear. "You can hear me now?" he asked.

"Yes!" said Eusebio, exasperated.

"Listen," the Bishop said, and sent him away. Eusebio joined the rest of us at the backstop.

Some kind of signal passed between the Bishop and Cleophas. At home plate Cleophas, who swears that none of these things I tell took place on my wedding day, pushed his sombrero off his head and onto his back. He drew his gun out of the holster. He wanted us to see him. He waited until we did.

He raised the Colt into the air and fired.

I shouted at him, "You said—"

"He lied! He lied!" said the Bishop, who knew. He was full of joy and amazement again. Ecstatic. An angel. He took half a windup. He seemed to check second base over his shoulder. He pitched his full ring of keys over the backstop and across the street. They struck the steps of the church.

One day in late December, Mrs. V picked Frank up early from school and took him away to the egg lady, a stranger you understand, but an angel. Mrs. V asked her to hide him at her place, and said that she would come back for him in two days. Instead, two days later, Mrs. V sent a message with a set of directions, which the angel read and followed.

Frank and his mother and the angel moved to a ranch on the *malpaís*, twenty miles southwest of Las Almas but as remote from it as on the moon. My mother said the *malpaís* was the place of terrible cures where plants like the golden mal de ojos could blind you or cure your blindness. Their own dead plant limbs are scattered around the starved ocotillo and cholla there. I was allowed to visit Frank there once a month on one of Willa Hancock's bays named Moyó. I brought Frank homework for the rest of the school year. I brought a hand-tooled saddlebag that Willa gave to Frank. He taught me to declaim in the way he did when he recited at school, and I impressed Cecilia Chamuscado with my new skill. Frank and his mother had to keep my visits to the *malpaís* secret. Only these two priests came to Mrs. V: my mother and Mrs. Gamboa. The three women prayed, shared food and drink, blessed one another.

Mr. V hunted Mrs. V. He owned a gun, but his rage was an unconcealed weapon. He asked everywhere about his son. "My Frank!" At our front door, he pounded the door frame loose with his fists. "My son is mine!" he said.

He begged for the priests' and the parish members' help in finding his wife and son, and he came again to my father and mother, and expected mercy, more money. He lost his job at the Stahmann pecan orchards. Our family, he said, was the cause of everything. Why had our family cursed his family in this way? From the law Mr. V uselessly demanded justice, and from God he received it, becoming an outcast and going almost mad.

I have walked enough of the path of madness to know by instinct the rest of the way. I believe Mr. V traveled all the darknesses in himself down to the drowning ones. I believe he would have gone mad if not for Mrs. Alcedama, I believe this truly.

At the risk of everyone's righteous indignation, Mercedes Alcedama visited Mr. V at his new adobe home. She made an offer. If he would work for the Alcedamas as caretaker of their plum and fig and pecan trees and gardens and rose gardens and grounds, she would instruct Mr. V in music, even buy him a guitar.

I have seen this guitar. Frank showed me. Mariachi guitar. Enormous. Key heads made of bone. Palest blond wood, black lightning trim on the edging and soundhole.

Beautiful guitar, I have stolen you every time I have remembered you.

Holding this instrument, more beautiful and of greater girth than it needed to be, the polished skin, the smooth, long neck, the curves I could rest my shoulder and head against, I wanted to have it.

By the new year, Mercedes Alcedama began to teach Mr. V to read. By that July, he had begun to learn to write. Mr. V, whose unlearned ancestors for three centuries had been unable to sign their names, and for two more centuries unable to write more than their names, learned to write words and sentences. The rock is placed across the entrance to the tomb, but it will be pushed aside. For a man it will be pushed aside. Was Mrs. V given a guitar? Was she given books? What waves of sound came into her home from a radio? What crumbs of hope was she offered? What ordained priests came?

Frank had the unsent letters his father wrote to him and his mother from 1925 to 1933, the year in which Frank was ordained a priest. Hundreds of pages of beauty. Frank has shown me them, the strange roots and weak, bare limbs of love's new growth.

RONDAS

The first night of the first week in Advent in 1995 I sold Christmas trees with Eusebio Gruber.

A miracle, truly. A year earlier when he was away, he had entrusted me to be caretaker of his land and home. How did I manage such a great responsibility? I pirated all his properties and gave them as a gift to the People. When he returned from his long trip, his wine (good wine), food, and clothes, three closetsful (old, new, and almost new), were gone. In his carpets were the footpaths and in his many books were the fingermarks of strangers. By then, his guard poodles had known too much love from too many children and so they guarded nothing anymore.

You will ask me, "Red, why would Eusebio let you—*you*—sell Christmas trees with him?"

Because he had forgiven me once, he could forgive me again. Because I was a sinner twice, I was twice-close to Christ. My teachers taught me this in Catholic grade school, and they taught Eusebio the same, and Recita and Cecilia. And the Bishop, he was taught the same. The path to salvation is sin. The best disciples were the prostitutes and tax evaders and thieves who hung near the Outlaw Christ and with Him and, at the last, next to Him.

Eusebio asked, "Will Recita come?" He was fearful, I could see. Like a man trying to see a great distance through a small, dim window, he looked at me for help.

"She is a good person," I said, but I knew this, her goodness, offered Eusebio no consolation at all.

He said, "She loves you? She loves you. She does."

"You can tell? You can tell," I said. "You can." I could have sung it, that is how happy it made me to say it! I am a man who likes to know from other men what I am feeling.

Once, on the first day I was caretaker for the Bonnar mansion on the east mesa, Mrs. Bonnar's brother asked me a question which was no question at all: "Do you plan to cheat us?" There were many ways to cheat them, many small things in their twelve rooms they would never miss, many irreplaceable treasures they did not treasure as I would. I definitely planned to cheat them. And it gave me such pleasure to hear him say it that I said, "Oh, yes!" I was fired. He shook my hand warmly before he let me out of the great house.

Eusebio settled a little in his lawn chair. I asked him the Big Questions. I asked, "Is this good? Do you worry?"

"Worry?" he said.

I said, "About you and me in business together. Do you worry?"

He said, "Red, you should be thankful you have wronged me before."

"I am," I said.

His rusted chair creaked. "What are the odds you will wrong me again?"

"Good," I said.

"Good," he said.

We both remembered Sister María Josefa telling all of us children that we must be thankful for our misfortune as well as our good fortune. We believed. Should we not have believed? We were second-graders. We are in our eighties today, and not as innocent, of course, but still foolish in our faith. Sister María Josefa, now an ex-Carmelite ex-teacher, is not as foolish in her faith but is still so innocent that people call her eccentric. Ninety-seven years old.

The first time Eusebio forgave me—before I pirated his home—it was for stealing his Christmas tree sales money. I stole all the profits he had raised for the St. Albert the Great church. I stole his penance. With this act of charity he had wanted to ransom his soul from a sin for which he could find no forgiveness even after the Bishop gave him absolution. So, you can see, his choice was clear about what he should do about me now: he should invite me to sell trees with him again.

Customers arrived at the iron gates of the cemetery where we sold the trees. We let them in. We closed the gates behind us. (Respectful. Not good for business, but respectful.) We had dug fencepost holes for the trees, and they leaned in the holes the way the gravestones leaned and the way the small white fences around the graves leaned and the plastic geraniums and daffodils, and the towering figure of La Virgen de Guadalupe, and the way we leaned forward because we were old men, the live wood in us warping. Here, the dead play *las rondas* and laugh at the living, who do not know they are playing *las rondas,* too.

Do you know the game? The children make a circle, or a circle inside a circle. You sing some nonsense rhyme, and then choose a child and say what she will be. Priest? President? Pope! Nun? Nurse? Musician! Magician! Mortician. If the child you have chosen likes the life you have chosen for her, she goes to the center. You say a nonsense rhyme.

¿Qué quiere usted?
Matarile rile rile

¿Qué quiere usted?
Matarile rile rile ron.

Matarile rile rile ron is a joyful meaninglessness, like saying "Eenie meenie minie mo." It is a way to sing without wanting to say, without needing to mean. How it feels to be an angel is no different than how it feels to be a child singing nonsense.

This is the place, here with these stones encircling stones, where Cecilia found peace after illness and long suffering. I had no story, no enchantment, and no rhyme that could revive her. Part of her wanted life; part wished for death. Two kinds of love. The gate should be closed on our griefs and memories here, and we should play again, like children. The dead would have it that way. The living should.

This was the right place to sell Christmas trees. If we did not sell them in this cemetery, where would we sell them? They were wrecked, ugly, feeble trees, and whatever cursed forest they came from, they should have been sent back to.

There in the cemetery, the customers somehow saw fresh, lovely, youthful, upright wonders—a miracle, no?—and they asked each other, "What tree is this? Where from?" They oohed and aahed and whistled and they leaned into each other and kissed and huddled in the trees' horrible shadow and, finally, they asked, "How much?"

"Fourteen bucks," Eusebio said, a born businessman.

There were price tags on all of the trees. All of them were fourteen bucks. But, still, people asked how much. Okay, yes, most of the customers were Catholics, the worst lost of all God's lost tribes. And, yes, some of them were Sister María Josefa's students and the children of the children of her students and all twice-close to Christ and too, too forgiving.

We sold another old couple a tree, the trunk peeling, the branches raining dry needles.

We walked the old ones and their sorrowful tree out of the gate. There a sentry appeared. The Bishop. He congratulated our customers. "Magnificent!" he said. He drew his open hands along the bottom and up the sides to the top of their tree, like he was drawing a triangle. He looked with love at the tree, and at his own fingertips which had touched the tree, and at the woman, the man. Do you know a blessing or a prayer with such power as this kind of touching? Did one needle fall when he caressed this tree? No. And as the people left, the cold breeze could not scatter the wide path of needles the tree shed. This touching was the Bishop's gift. I call him the Bishop because he was once and because I will not forget. Our Mother Church expels her children for the sins you and I would lose in one wipe of a rag across a table and one shrug and two unbinding words, "Forget it."

After the man honked and the woman waved from behind the car window, I asked the Bishop this one-word question: "Magnificent?"

"Magnificent!" he said.

"You are a liar, Frank."

"Am I?" he asked.

He had not brought a lawn chair as Eusebio and I had, and he looked at our card table to gauge whether it would hold him, which of course it would, since he was slight, slight as all ancient dust that will soon become the breath of stars.

"Good setup," the Bishop said. He sat on the edge. "We are in the Business, Eusebio." He said—I think he said this to the trees or to the gravestones or to me—he said, "They will come now." He rested more of his weight on the table. "'Advent' means this: 'They will come.'"

"I am not so sure," said Eusebio.

"Me either," I said. "It means: 'He—Christ—will come.' Right?" Unordained but catechized by Sister María Josefa, I knew what I knew.

"Watch," said the Bishop. "Keep watch." He scooted up onto the table, not a high table at all. His feet dangled above the ground, his black bishop's shoes swung, his red Albertson's Superstore jacket flapped against his chest, the only sign that a breeze visited us.

"Knock, knock" came a voice at the gate, and another, "Anybody home?"

The Bishop launched himself. Before his feet struck the ground, he hovered. He hummed. He hummed and he hovered. You can ask Eusebio if you will not believe. The Bishop delivered the customers onto our sales floor, which was our cemetery showroom. "It is Elizabeth Yarrow. Elizabeth! And Recita!" he said as if he never saw them both in church every Sunday for seventy years. Recita hugged him and hugged me, and held me against her, and pivoted with me and suddenly sat down in my chair. "Hah!" she said. Liz giggled. We called Elizabeth Yarrow Liz Why when we were children. We boys called her Liz When in high school because she was so stubbornly chaste. She married Lou Oczpyswyski in 1930 and then we called her Liz What? and him Lou What? And even Liz and Lou enjoyed the joke because friends rib, you know, and when Lou died as a soldier somewhere east of the Rhine in March 1945, it eased the loss to have the joke, this is the truth.

Liz said, "Oh dear, dear Eusebio," and touched the front of his stocking cap with both her hands, "and my dear Francisco. And Red—you are here, too, Red?"

What could I answer? Recita answered for me: "A miracle."

Eusebio said, "A miracle."

The Bishop said, "They will erect a shrine here someday!"

Recita now looked at Eusebio, who had gazed steadily at her to invite her scrutiny. She asked, "You have room for us, Eusebio?"

He knew what she was asking. He opened his eyes wider

so she might find the answer. He drew both his fists to his heart. Here he had found room. She could see. We all could.

She touched the front of his stocking cap in the way Liz had done.

"I have news," Liz said. But she did not offer her news. She looked at the four of us and at the pitiful trees and the light fog silvering the cemetery darkness beyond our flashlight lighting up our sign: Eusebio's Christmas Trees. She said, "I will help you sell trees."

"That is your news?" I asked.

"These trees are magnificent, no?" said the Bishop.

Eusebio said, "Liz, the cold is hard on you, how will you stand it?"

"You will help," she said.

"I will?" he asked.

And how did he hear her so well? He heard her perfectly.

Liz stood behind Eusebio, resting her hands on the back of his lawn chair. She had no gloves. The sleeves of her green vinyl coat were too short for her arms, and her wrists and hands were bare. Standing next to Recita, I noticed how Liz moved her dark hands onto Eusebio's shoulders, spread her fingers into the clean cloth of his wool coat. "I can help," she said quietly, one fingernail digging for Eusebio's special attention. "Santa Spray Snow." Her fingers scored his chest and again she named the trinity: "Santa. Spray. Snow."

"What?" said Eusebio.

"Santa. Spray. Snow."

"That is your news?" I asked.

Recita said, "Be quiet and listen, Red." She placed my warm hands on her bare neck. I looked to see where she had put her purse, I don't know why.

"If you spray Santa Snow on the trees," Liz said, "you will improve sales."

"How?" asked Eusebio.

"Amazing!" said the Bishop.

"I will spray them," she said. "People like a real tree to have fake snow on it." Liz's fingernail did not dig now. It rubbed a circle into the dampness on Eusebio's coat, a new coat, and probably expensive. "It makes the tree look more— real—or something," she said. "And it preserves the tree."

"Yes!" The Bishop loved this idea of making our awful trees more awful.

"Yes," said Recita. Her purse was on the Bishop's lap.

"The fake snow smells minty, like inside candy canes," Liz said.

"Well," said Eusebio.

Liz's hands moved away, her palms turned out, her fingers curved up as if she held rosaries. So many times, my mother had done this the same way. All of this silent blessing happened and was over in an instant. "Yes?" she asked.

The Bishop and I already knew Eusebio's answer. What harm done to these damned trees could damn them more?

She said, "Three dollars and five cents a can. I will buy the cans. And a surgical mask. And a big hairbrush. I need forty dollars." Eusebio drew the money from his front left pocket. Lincoln. Lincoln. Hamilton. Jackson. She explained that she would receive two dollars for every snowy tree we sold, and she would pay the cost for the Santa Spray Snow at the end of Advent.

"Here," said Eusebio. He pulled his gloves off. "Will you wear them?" he asked. He asked for her hand, which she gave him, saying, "Yes, I will." He fit the wool over her dark, gnarled fingers. He smoothed the leather palm with his own bare palm. The glove exactly matched the coat. You can see that a man like Eusebio does not live as we live, even if he once did. When we were children he and all of us played *rondas* together, standing in a circle, making up nonsense songs, spinning words to see them spin. We were from poor families. What else could we spend but our words, our voices?

He fit the other glove to Liz's other hand.

"Will you have them?" asked the Bishop, who, like me, believed in acts of charity with other people's property.

"I will," she said.

"Wonderful!" said the Bishop, and he slapped Eusebio's back and patted his shoulders, calming the eddies there.

"Bless you," she said. She accepted money. Recita slipped away from me, and followed her. The light fog closed behind and over Recita like veil lace.

Eusebio said, "Liz is a believer." She was gone now, and he felt safe to talk about her. Old men will talk this way about the women. There is no stopping it.

"Do you remember Miss Iffrig?" he asked. "Liz was one of her pets. Remember?"

Who could forget? Miss Iffrig, high school Latin, who believed—in truth, sincerely believed—she was the reincarnation of Gaius Julius Caesar's horse. She wore toga dresses interstitched with elaborate ribbon harnesses over the shoulders and under and between her breasts. We were fifteen and we, the boys, we noticed. The girls noticed too. If she noticed that we noticed, it made no difference to her, except that it caused her to laugh sometimes when the lust and wonder swam together to the surface of our eyes. She told us that what we would learn from her about Caesar's Gallic campaigns came from her direct experience.

"Liz *believed*," said Eusebio.

"Me too!" said the Bishop.

We knew. We knew he believed. Did he still believe?

Miss Iffrig whinnied when she laughed, baring her huge teeth. She tossed her gray mane, and, to get our attention, she stamped her foot. Her glasses had long chains that hung down from her cheeks and over her neck. Powerful, thick neck.

In class she made us recite from memory the Passages for

Translation and Comprehension. She interrupted and corrected us. "Declaim!" she said.

Eusebio declaimed badly. He recited each word like a sacred poker chip. "*Alea*—" He anted, "*Alea*," he raised, "*Alea*," he raised again. "*Iacta?*" He was a bluffer, not a declaimer. "*Est?*" He would be a businessman, a merchant. This was clear, even then.

Recita declaimed boldly and so quickly she could not be questioned. It did not make her proud to learn things, it made her proud to *know*. This made her a bad student and a good hospital nurse, beloved for thirty-five years at Memorial where they have put up a plaster bust of her that she says is too big in the bust. The male patients loved her. It is said that many male patients loved her. Recita herself has said to me, "I never once felt the need of marriage," and I have said, "Right!" and we are both old enough to laugh at all that myth and history. She helped raise sixteen children whose mothers all needed a Tía Mama. Her four older sisters each had four children who are loyal to and loving toward her, and who have given her who knows how many godchildren—twelve at least. They never hold still to be counted—but twelve, I think.

I always sat in the same row, with Cecilia sitting behind and Recita ahead of me. I declaimed good as Cicero but I mispronounced. I was passionate and convincing and incorrect. Miss Iffrig called me "Sicarius," the Assassin. I would be a pirate of one kind or another. Real estate or clothing or car salesman. Or worse.

"Francisco," she said, "declaim!" and already the slight diamond-shaped depression in her forehead blushed because Frank *could declaim*. Wonderfully. Wonderfully. "*Alea iacta est.*" A wind inside him tore the words from their slender black branches in our textbook. Angry wind. Conquering wrath. Offering mercy. Merciless. The words whistled in their flight.

"The die is cast." He could declaim. Like a mayor or a radio personality, like a priest who might, with God's grace, become a bishop.

Miss Iffrig closed her eyes, dark eyes from which an untamed deeper darkness could always appear. Her neck and shoulders shivered as he recited the account of crossing the Rubicon.

Outside school some of us said: She might be. She might be.

We were divided unevenly into those who said *might* and those who said *is*. Unbelievers and believers. Francisco Velasco, Liz When, and Cecilia Chamuscado said *is*. (Eusebio and Liz were sweet on each other.)

I was not a Believer, but to interest Cecilia in me, I said that, in time, I could become a Believer. Frank heard about this from Cecilia. He asked me: "No lie?" Discovering in that very instant that the lie might deepen our friendship, I said, "No lie." Here is my advice to all naturally dishonest, solitary boys and men: To steal love, inspire irrational fervor.

Liz and Recita returned with an Albertson's plastic shopping basket full of Santa Snow Spray and other equipment. Recita took my chair again.

Liz and Eusebio designated which trees she would spray. She put on her white gauze mask. In the darkness, she leaned the trees toward her in their fencepost holes, turning them, snowing over them with the spray can pointed up. With the big hairbrush she brushed out clumps of white on branches that rained needles and broke away at the slightest touch. Her gloves slowly turned white, the gloves of Eusebio, and then her green vinyl coat and her bare wrists. She wheezed and sang "Adeste Fidelis" through the mask. Her singing was bright, and the lilting parts were somehow more alluring through the mask: *Venita adoremus, Venite adoremus, Venite adoremus Dominum.*

When her safety glasses were completely coated, she worked blind, a glittering mist around her. Eusebio and the Bishop and I stared. Appreciating. Appreciating. Old men, you know: the bottle has been shaken, but not all the Tabasco is gone.

Recita was the first to notice we had new customers. "Boys," she said, "pay attention."

"See who comes," the Bishop said.

Arlene, Faye, and Altadena. What were the chances of this—that Liz Why and Arlene, Faye, and Altadena would visit on the same Advent night? But they did. They stepped through the fog and through the mist of the spray snow and, as miracles should, they shone like salt spilled upon a silver tray. They held each other's hands. When Recita opened her arms to them, they closed her in their circle without letting go of each other.

They looked at us, at Liz, at our snowy and unsnowy trees.

Faye said, "Lovely." She held one hand over her bowler hat as if the loveliness she saw might blow it from her head.

Arlene said, "Too much beautiful."

"You got a problem," said Altadena, "do you know?" The three sisters crowded around our table. They smelled good. I liked how they smelled. I can't remember: How did they smell?

The three sisters, triplets, were very different, though they wore their blue hair in the same way, with a pale blue pentecostal flame teased up from their low foreheads. They were much loved in our valley, these sisters, but I wondered if people would like them better wearing fake snow; if it would preserve them. They smelled minty.

"Wonderful!" said the Bishop. "We have *one* problem? And no others?"

"Serious problem," said Altadena. "We can help."

The three old sisters wore red Christmas bowlers on their heads, the expensive kind, wine red, and very old, and probably the spray snow would not come off them.

"You can see we have help," said Eusebio.

Arlene said, "And customers?"

"And customers," said Eusebio.

"And no problems?" asked Faye.

"None," said Eusebio.

"Until now," said Altadena. "Sheriff Morales. He says you have no permit. He plans to shut you down." Someone told me once that Altadena was the firstborn of the three, that she gave some kind of okay for Faye to follow and then Arlene.

"This is true?" Eusebio asked Faye. Her son was Sheriff Morales.

"True," said Faye.

"Sheriff Morales is too good. Too honorable," said Arlene. "It is a problem." She patted Faye's back to console her for the unfortunate virtues of her son.

"Faye has the Influence," said Altadena.

We laughed, the Bishop, Eusebio, me, Recita, Arlene, Faye, because there are pleasures in the inevitabilities that, truly, only people our age can appreciate.

Altadena did not laugh. Her jaw tightened. Her lower lip seemed to taste something on her upper lip. "We are here to sell the Influence."

"Does this need to be explained?" asked Faye.

"We will explain," said Arlene.

"Please," said Eusebio.

Altadena said, "We may take your chairs?"

We stood. They sat.

"Thank you," Altadena said. "How it is, is this. Faye has the Influence and can tell Sheriff Morales to stay away. She will tell him—if you permit us to sell decorations for the Bell Fund."

"The Bell Fund," I said. "Of course!"

"Of course," said Eusebio. "The Bell Fund."

The Bishop said, "The Bell Fund!"

"Simple, no?" said Altadena.

The diocese had supported the Bell Fund when Frank had been the Bishop. The new bishop thought it was frivolous, and the fund-raising stopped. The problem was that Christ Is King church had bells, fake bells, and a tape recording of real bells, and plenty of us believed that was not the same at all. When the Bell Fund began, the parish members learned that our bell tower was a fake tower, and that a new tower, even a humble one, would cost what whole churches once cost, and that real bells had no *campanero*, no bell ringer, now, but were on complicated automated systems, expensive, and unreliable.

Fake bells were not the same, people said, but many were discouraged about the money. Some asked if we should not get a different tape recording of bells, New Mexico bells, and not the bells of a church in Asheville, North Carolina. Some asked if a better sound system would help.

No, no, no, said the sisters Úbeda, and made this speech: "The real sound is sacred. The real tower must tower. The tradition of the bell keepers must return. We vow it."

This was their speech, and after making it they made the sign of the cross, slowly, and in unison, and made an appeal for a specific large amount of money, and if you considered saying no for one second, well, you had them there before you, all three of them, and they explained that a monthly payment program was acceptable, and you would receive visits from each of them soon to tell you more about it, because they had vowed, and they must keep their vows, you understand, of course you do, because God has called you to make vows too, and you must persist in them, no?

An hour later, they returned to the cemetery to sell their goods with us. Liz Why, who had been watching all along, watching, watching—she was pleased. The lace-and-sugar bells and snowflakes would be blessings on her white trees, she said.

They brought the bleached white lambswool that could be placed under the trees. They brought white felt ribbon knotted into angels the size of thumbs, and father and mother and child angels the size of hands. These angels and angel families were Altadena's creations. Faye and Arlene had ingeniously devised lace-covered dry yucca pods; the seeds in them rattled at the slightest touch. A set of ten was twenty dollars. A set of twenty was fifty.

Liz and the sisters set up a model tree next to our table. They decorated it with the white lace creations, placed the lambswool underneath, hung the yucca bells, and topped the tree with a dry yucca branch, its upraised arms full of lace-covered pods. We touched the tree to hear it rattle. Needles rained down. Spray snow fell in clumps.

"We will make a killing," said Arlene, the last born, and the quietest one, not the one with the nerve, not the one with the Influence.

Faye said, "I must telephone him."

"Yes, you must," said Altadena, and all three left together again to make their phone call to Sheriff Morales from the Albertson's pay phone. They walked through Liz's spray snow mist. She waved. She bowed, and made the tree she was snowing upon bow too. In the moonlight the two small shadows, tree and woman, darted out onto the ground and disappeared. In the game of *rondas* we had said she would be a nun.

When we could, we children played *rondas* in the moonlight in order to see the future in our faint shadows. We sang.

¿Qué quiere usted?
Matarile rile rile
¿Qué quiere usted?
Matarile rile ron.

Yo escojo a Cecilia
Matarile rile rile
Yo escojo a Cecilia
Matarile rile ron.

After the sisters left, we talked about them. I said I liked Arlene best. Recita stretched her legs out, and modestly arranged her long skirt. I envied her the chair. She said, "Arlene was Cecilia's favorite."

Eusebio said sadly, "The sisters Úbeda. They look rich. People think so. But they are poor. So poor."

"They give good confessions," said the Bishop. He guarded his mouth with his folded hands. "I cannot tell," he said. "I wish I could."

There was an indecent unsilent silence while his memory and our imaginations combusted.

"Shame on you," said Recita.

"Tell a little," said Eusebio.

The Bishop said, "No. No." But he shrugged. He was no longer a bishop, after all. He shrugged again. "I liked Altadena's confessions best."

Our breathing made the sound of streams joining. I repeated, "I liked Arlene best."

Eusebio said nothing. The Bishop hummed. Hummed. He said, "Eusebio always liked Liz Why. True, Eusebio?"

Eusebio tapped his pink hearing aid. "I hear humming," he said.

I looked over at Liz. By now, I knew she would cover all the trees in snow. She was a force of nature. Arlene, Faye, Altadena: they were, too. Miss Iffrig. Sister María Josefa. Cecilia Chamuscado. Recita Holguín.

I said I remembered how dearly Cecilia had loved all the sisters. The four shared a bicycle, the one bicycle of the sisters. They shared Cecilia's kites made by her famous uncle Liston

Potter, famous for gambling and drinking, and famous for making butcher-paper kites, as if that made up for all the rest. (We heard the litany from Cecilia's mother every kite season: Liston, who saws his stupid fiddle. Liston, who throws his money in the sewer. Liston, the No Good Butcher Bum. Liston, the Kite Maker!)

Cecilia, Recita, Arlene and Faye and Altadena shared one real, unmatched whole tea set and a small, round serving table and faded violet tablecloth they had collected from *tíos, abuelos,* and *abuelas.* Cecilia told me. Beneath a cluster of three old apple trees, they excluded boys and welcomed girls to their tea ceremonies, which were as Japanese and British and exotic India as they could possibly imagine, and which were part Catholic Mass and part pajama party, and part *rondas.*

"Cecilia invited me once," the Bishop said.

I said nothing. Eusebio said nothing. The Bishop was never a good liar. I thought this was a grand lie. I would give him time to take it back: an obligation among old, good friends.

Without asking out loud, I asked Recita for the truth. She answered, "He's right."

He said, "I was not supposed to tell."

The sisters returned with three paper cups of coffee, three chocolate reindeer wrapped in gold foil, three purple candles and one rose-colored.

Three customers arrived with them. The sisters Úbeda had recruited them at Albertson's.

"A night of miracles!" said the Bishop, who would say this anyway, even if it wasn't true, but who spoke truly now. They were our classmates! If we had planned a class reunion, how could we ever have so many together? The lost souls of the living. Eleven of us. The souls of so many others resting in the Christ Is King church cemetery. Like children playing *ron-das*, we were a circle within a circle again.

"Agnes!" I said but we all said it then, "Agnes!" and said, "Libby!" and said, "Margaret Loving Middleton!" Her name came complete from us, and you can see that such music would.

Liz (watching, watching) pulled her mask down onto her neck. "My Lord and God!" she said, her words making pale flowers in the light fog and spray snow mist surrounding her.

Now there was the hugging, kissing on the foreheads and the cheeks. Unashamed, we held each other's hands, we touched each other's arms and heads. Las Almas is a small community and we sometimes saw each other, of course we did, but never together. Liz hugged onto all of us, hugged herself around the cluster of hugging people, marking us with the fake snow covering her.

I wept. My nose ran. Everyone offered something for me to blow into. When I finished, Recita kissed my runny nose.

Margaret Loving Middleton kissed the Bishop's finger where a bishop's ring had once been. He kissed her finger where her wedding rings had been. Margaret took away her hand. "Is something wrong?" she asked him. The water of his eyes was troubled. He kissed her, then, square on the lips. Not unchaste. Not chaste.

Who knows what stones the heart rolls away? His kiss made me wonder what was in his mind, and it made me remember he had said, "Cecilia invited me once," and "I was not supposed to tell," and it made me think of everything he had not said yet.

Our arms were falling away now, and our hands. We stood close enough to embrace, our white breaths like spokes around Liz Why, who had moved from the outside to the center of our circle.

I blurted out a question. "Did you believe?" As if it made anything clearer, I asked, "Were you believers?"

Arlene said, "You dear man," which was a kind way to ask me to explain. Do you know a kinder way?

"Miss Iffrig," I said. "Miss Iffrig. Did you believe? Were you a *might*—or *is?*"

"She was a horse," said Arlene.

"Caesar's horse," said Faye.

"Body and spirit," said Altadena, who nudged me to the center.

"*Sí,*" said Liz.

The game of *rondas* has a form. The form was second nature to us all.

"*Sí.*"

"Caesar's horse."

Our dead schoolmates seemed to be with us now. The whole circle of spirits.

"Horse."

"Absolutely! Caesar's. Caesar's." Oidora Zorita.

"Magnificent horse!" Pete Bustamante.

"Horse. *Sí.*" Jay Lydeck.

"Horsey. See? *Sí.*" Philipa Oroz.

"Caesar's." Albert Ulloa.

"Caesar's!" The Bishop.

"Caesar's." Purísima Beaumont.

"Caesar's horse." P. Z. Abert.

"*Sí.*" Isidro Peralta.

"*Sí.*" Eusebio Gruber.

"*Veni.*"

"*Vidi.*"

"*Vici.*"

Gus Hillers. Mark Vetancurt. Laurencia Guerra.

"*Sí.*"

Our schoolmates and the ghosts of schoolmates were there. All but one. All but Cecilia. And they were all *is*. No *might*s. And I an unbeliever. "You believed?" I asked.

"Why do you want to know?" asked the Bishop, who took my place at the center of the circle, who placed me next to Faye.

"Because," I said, "Cecilia believed."

"Body and spirit," said Altadena.

"You are thinking of Cecilia?" asked the Bishop. How clearly he asked it. My friend all my life. My confessor. He stood at the center. There is a form in the Mass that makes possible the transubstantiation; in the confessional that offers absolution; in the final blessing that promises salvation. There is a form in eighty years of friendship that decides what will be said and must be left unsaid.

The Bishop said, "I am thinking of her, too." His eyes closed and his head moved as if he would find a certain perfume in the cold around him. He declaimed: "Cecilia Chamuscado. Cecilia Chamuscado." She could be—could she not?—called out of the graveyard fog into our arms again, to kiss my open mouth and his wet eyes.

There is a form. The Bishop stood at the center. If I wanted, I could ask: What is the greater sin? That Cecilia loved a priest or that she loved two men?

But—I knew the answers. She loved me. She loved him.

Margaret and Agnes and Liz, Faye and Arlene and Altadena, all had been at the tea ceremonies. The circle of spirits encircling the Bishop knew, all knew, already knew how he loved Cecilia. Sinning against his God and Church and friend, he loved her. Awful and beautiful truth. Not more awful than beautiful.

"See?" Faye asked. A light from the street shined through our white trees and over our small table and upon our childish circle. When the golden light stopped moving, when it rested on Faye, it rolled the fog into a golden cave. She stood at the mouth of the cave. Our circle divided into two curved lines behind her. Faye peered into the cave, the long path. She reached up with both hands, removed her wine-red bowler, her blue hair afire, so little hair really, so much light. To give her son a signal, she held the hat before her like a beggar, tilted it until it filled.

In 1933, at the beginning of Advent, Mrs. V agreed to meet her husband again in Gamboa's.

They had not seen each other for almost ten years.

My mother served them water and coffee when she collected their menus. She told my father and me this, and told us of what she prayed into the water and coffee. (Ark of Peace. Mother of God. Fountain of Heaven.) She told us how Mrs. and Mr. Velasco sat together at the table, one next to the other. Elizabeth and Antonio. Thirty-one years after their marriage, their courtship began according to Elizabeth's will.

Elizabeth asked Antonio to tell her what she already knew: about the reading, the music, the husbanding of orchards and gardens. How was it possible for Elizabeth to stay there and listen to the waves of joy that poured from him? How was it possible for her to forgive him? Such love is the mystery all faith is built upon and the burden all faith collapses under. Have you known such love?

After the miracle of the reunion of Elizabeth and Antonio Velasco, my mother gave no sign of grieving when my father strayed from the Faith. He took this as permission from his one true pastor and confessor, and he strayed more often. We both did.

God was involved in all that, you see. God must have been, for hadn't my mother schemed for my father and me to eat the blessed bread and the blessed lemonade that worked terrible and wonderful miracles in the Velasco family? Didn't we both, son and father, thief and heretic, eat the bread and drink from the cup, and remain unchanged? God was involved, surely God was.

The Bishop was right when he said God's plots are weird. The Bishop knew.

They are gone now, my mother and father.

You are gone, Mother and Father, and what you have left me I trace my hand along. My pieces of paper. Finer than onion skin.

ASK THE OWL ABOUT THE DARKNESS

Tears come too easy, and I cry at almost anything. My eyes and nose water. A dripping man.

Today in Recita's bathtub I philosophized. What is Misery? I asked myself. I do this, ask the Big Questions, and cannot help doing this. I cannot make a Plan, have never been able to make one, but my mind draws maps to all the shores where I cannot land.

I was reading the newspaper, the *Las Almas Sun-News,* in the bath, trying to keep the water and the words from mixing. I could hear myself reading out loud but I was reading only inside myself.

> *Fr. Francisco Velasco, former bishop of the Catholic Diocese of Las Almas, died Sunday morning in his apartment in Anthony.*

I miss how it felt to be a boy reading out loud to my parents.

> *Funeral and burial services will be held at Christ Is King church cemetery.*

My father used to say, "You are better than radio, boy." For a man who revered the waves as he did, this compliment was almost sacrilege. My father has been gone for fifty years and my mother for twenty, and I should have outgrown missing them. *El que vive en el recuerdo nunca muere.* The person who is remembered never dies.

All contributions should be made to the Christ Is King Christmas Tree Campaign.

Inside me, words echoed over knives, and blood and language blended. I thought of funnel cakes, white and black petticoats, lace-and-sugar snowflakes, a comb in a plastic case, a pack of gum, a Parker pen, an egg slicer and a giant sign, an Advent wreath, empty purse, empty holster, an empty flask. At the bathroom door, Recita said, "Red. I have an idea." She is my bride, we are newlyweds. We have been married four months.

She holds up a handbrush and a hard, gray bar of soap. The way she is dressed is how she dresses at night. Tantalizing. In bed, Recita wears black nylon running shorts over her old woman's underwear, which is bigger than the running shorts and shows through. Her legs are bare, lovely all the way up. On top she wears one of my sleeveless white T-shirts but under it a light blue filmy, sexy, brand-new something that would be see-through if I could see through the T-shirt. At night Recita guides my hands over the layers of bed sheets and under one layer of clothing at a time. If she invites me in, she takes the layers off. But then she puts them back on. Under the sheets, she slowly rewraps herself. She will not allow me to touch her hair. I may touch her ears, her neck, her brow, but I may not touch her hair.

She says, "You need polishing."

I have never been polished. "Polish me," I say.

She holds up the gray brick. "You will like this."

"Polish me."

She kneels by the side of the bathtub. She sands my balding head with the brick. She scrubs with the brush, and sands my whole neck with the soap brick, and not lightly. "Sting?" she asks.

"Stings good," I say, because I am a newlywed and feel the obligation.

She says, "You have a dull back, very dull." She gives it the treatment. It needs more treatment, I guess, because she does not relent.

I ask, "Am I still dull?"

"Is that a mole?" she asks, attacking the mole on my back with her brick, her brush, her fingernail.

"It is a mole," she says. "Sorry."

I must stand up for part of the treatment, the worst, best part.

And then. Almost done with me, she says, "You will like this." She runs more water in the bath.

"How do you know?" I ask, but why do I ask? I know she does this to herself, polishes herself. Under everything she wears, nothing is dull.

"Now," she says, "your feet." She unwraps herself of the T-shirt and the black running shorts and the old woman's underwear. She takes off her sexy brand-new see-through something. She climbs in opposite me and rests my feet in her lap. If I was not a newlywed and still afraid of my own married shadow I would say to her, "Your breasts are beautiful miseries," because they are, they are. Recita's breasts are her body's last ripenings and her nipples point straight down and her fallen deep-brown-red roundnesses float at her waist as beautiful as molten glass.

She threatens me: "If you stare, I'll dress." She sands my right foot. Who can believe a big brick of soap can be forced between the toes? It can.

"Dull," she says, giving my foot the treatment, resting it on the center of her chest, the hard board of bone there. "Ugly dust on top of uglier dust."

"Oh that," I say. "That is from my father's side of the family. Never comes off."

But she is determined. "Hurt?" she asks.

"Hurts good," I say. The obligation, you know.

An hour has passed. The bathwater is cold but relieving. We have kissed each other's feet, kissed and sung to and made puppet speeches and wrestling matches with each other's feet.

She stands up in the tub. Towers over me. Flowering cliff, ancient fountain, dripping old woman. During our courtship in Christ Is King church we stood and kneeled close to each other, singing, singing, and my skin singing—hers, too—I think hers, too—like the skin of a bell struck long ago and still ringing. When she leans over, as she never did in the church, to kiss my polished head and polished ears, her hair brushes me, her dripping hair, thick, with traces of silver, but black. I kiss the birthmark on the bridge of her nose, the dark fingerprint she says her Mexican ancestors put there when they visited her pregnant mother in a dream.

My toes hurt when I look at her. Tears come to my eyes. I ask, "May I polish you now?"

She says, "I do not need polishing, Red. I am almost new."

Is this Misery?

No. No.

Yesterday a package came from the Bishop, wrapped in thin white paper, smooth, waxed paper, but thin, and you could see the outline of Santa printed on its other side. Christmas paper the Bishop had saved. He was one of those conservers. In different corners of his apartment were piles of crushed cans, glass jars, plastic containers, newspapers. I asked him once about the tall piles and the congregation of bugs in the piles. "I am a priest," he said as if that was an answer.

"Oh, Frank," I said to this package in my hands. "No, Frank."

He had written his address, La Florida Deluxe Apartments, 517 S. Main, Anthony, New Mexico, in his small, bowing longhand letters, bowing except for the capitals. His *F* was like the prow of a ship. *F*rancisco. His longhand *V* had great curved wings: *V*elasco. When he was the Most Reverend Bishop of the Diocese of Las Almas, this *V* was his binding promise and his mark of blessing.

On the back of the package were five words in his hand:

I promised.
Fountain. Mother. Ark.

"What have you done?" I asked, and sat down at the kitchen table and put the package between my feet. The wrapping paper was the pagan kind. Santa was merry, very merry or jolly, and the golden smoke cloud from his pipe was festive or rosy or one of those words, you know which ones, canned as creamed corn. The golden reindeer behind him raised up their antlers in one joined Christmas crown.

Eight reindeer. I called them by name. Come, Dancer! Come, Prancer! I couldn't help myself. Come, Donner! Come, Blitzen! Like a sled, my memory wished to fly. Come, Cabeza de Vaca! Come, Don Juan de Oñate! To the top of the roof to the roof of the sky! Hail, Mary, and away!

Through the kitchen window I can see how the trumpet vines have overtaken one of our Mexican elder trees and smothered it, trunk, branch, and treetop, in orange bellflowers.

"What have you done?" I asked the package. But I knew what. The Bishop had cut all of his hair and sent it to keep a promise to my mother.

And he had blessed me one final time. "Fountain of Heaven. Mother of God. Ark of Peace" was his full blessing, old as our friendship.

I had his hair now. Where would I put the package?

I will put it near our bed.

Recita, she owes, you see, she owes her own hair, and does not complain about the mail, the hundreds of packages of hair that come from people who will not break the promise that they or someone they loved made to my mother. Our closets and cabinets are filled with the packages.

Our car. Our crawlspaces. Behind our sofa. Under our bed.

Home-dyed and just-permed hair, never washed and overwashed and wavy and hat-mashed and braided and helmet-crushed. Hairnetted and perfumed and invalid hair.

The hair smells like biscuits and like mayonnaise and refried beans and brown sugar and cake mix and licorice and birthday candles and pumpkin flesh. Like damp bread dough and diaper pails and Corona cerveza. Wherever the hands have been the hair has known. Whose hands never travel to his hair? The hair smells like votive candles, onion and chile fields, locker rooms. The hair feels like kisses had been kissed there or like it is unblessed, unkissed hair.

Recita and I sift the hair with our fingers. Over our kitchen table we spread the hair. No person forms there, no face or head or fine neck. You cannot make it form a picture, sign, or word. It is the spirit.

Sometimes a note might be enclosed. A week ago a package came with this: "*Cowlicks!*" No signature. No return address. How do I know if this hair is my responsibility. I have no list.

"*It was more curly than it looks.*"

"*It reached to her knees.*"

"*Not much here. This is all of it.*"

Oily and waxed and moussed and brittle and pony- and pigtailed and tied in a *chongo*. Sticky with blood and snagged with knots and sticks and grass and leaves and lint and flower petals. And herbs and vines and white roots and river moss and mud. And every shaft five hundred colors.

"Oh, Frank," I said, when I opened the package his hair came in. I spread it out, I started counting. The dark strands were so rough. He should have combed more often. He should have brushed it.

He loved a good story, a long confession, a serial confession of one sin leading to another and another. This pleased him.

When he was still a very young Basilian, thirty years old, I confessed to him about stealing again, about taking a man's shirts from his car, fine shirts, cleaned, heavy starch, white, all white, each one wrapped in waxed paper by One-Hour Cleaners. (I have the hair of Quirino McGee, the owner of One-Hour.)

The Bishop asked, "How many shirts?"

"Eight shirts."

He gave me my penance: eight Hail Marys.

"Is that enough?" I asked.

"White looks nice on you," he said. He noticed. Of course he noticed. He was my dearest friend. I was his.

I said, "Bless me."

He said, "Don't leave."

"There is a line," I said. If you are in the confessional a long time, the whole line behind you knows your sins are many or great, or many and great.

He left the confessional. I heard him push open his narrow door. "Go home," he said to the line. "You're forgiven."

There must have been some resistance to this. He said, "No kidding. I forgive you." He said, "Bow your heads. There. Your sins are forgiven. Sin no more."

We Catholics can be stubborn if our forgiveness seems lower than the current rate of exchange. He had to use the Latin on them: "*Dominus noster Jesus Christus te absolvat*"—all that, and said fast as lightning, "*In nomine Patris, et Filii et Spiritus Sancti.*"

When he returned, the Bishop closed the narrow door. He said, "Red. Start over." He had done this often, asked me to begin from the beginning, from the original sin.

I told how I had planned to steal the shirts. I knew the man picked up his shirts at noon on Mondays, I knew where he would park his car after he picked them up, that he would park at First National Bank on Missouri Street, eat lunch at the Golden Bull on Solano and Montana Streets, and not be able to see his car.

I planned how I would do it, and I prayed I would not. I planned when I would do it, and I prayed again that I would not. I sat in the man's car and prayed this prayer: "Why am I here?" I looked inside the waxed paper wrapping, and asked God, "Are they my size?" They looked my size.

When I left the car with the shirts, I slammed the car door. No one came. I walked past the Golden Bull in view of the man and of God and the smiling face of the bull, an old face, wise and approving. Ephpheta "Sugar" Salazar painted this face in 1936. I have the hair of her first three husbands, and I will have the hair of her fourth if I live long enough.

In the bathroom of the bank I tried on one of the white shirts, and looked hard into the mirror. Most of the shirts had two pockets. Button-down collars. I did not cry, but I coughed and could not catch my breath. I kneeled at the sink and ran the water into my hands and over my arms. I prayed the baptism prayer: that the unclean spirit depart from me. I imagined I felt his thumb, the thumb of the priest, draw the sign upon my forehead and my chest. "Receive the sign of the Cross both upon the forehead and also upon the heart that now thou mayest be the temple of God." I anointed my head in the running water of the First National Bank. I imagined I saw there in the sink a hairbrush, ring of keys, a white silk cord, fresh golden straw, a pirate flag, folding chair, featherweight Stetson, and a rag made from a child's undershirt. I imagined the priest reciting, "Give place to the Holy Ghost," and breathing into my face, three gentle breaths.

"The shame I felt! The shame was like fire." I did not look at the screen between us in the confessional. I looked in the pockets of my shirt. Each pocket had a button. Very nice.

"And?" he said.

I said, "That's all."

Did he hear? He said nothing.

"That's all," I said again. But it was not all.

He said, "Amazing," in a way that said, "There is more, no?"

"Okay," I said. What is Misery? What is Misery? "I burned with shame all night. I grew white hot, and cooled, and smoldered in my bed. I saw myself in my new shirts, walking upon a wide curving path of shining water. On the surface of the river was your face and the face of my mother and Cecilia, and the face of Recita. Deep beneath the surface, I saw the swimming figure of my father, a happy acrobat of the depths. In other words, I saw myself in heaven, where I would never be. Not ever."

"And?" the Bishop said.

"I burned to ashes. I fell asleep. I dreamed a wooden crucifix, a violet tablecloth, a child's toothbrush, a doghouse, a dog bowl, purple stole, red paint, a mirror, scissors, menu, missal, Mexican spur, and *Baltimore Catechism, Simplified with Explanations.*"

"Seventeenth edition?" he asked.

"Seventeenth."

This next part I did not want to tell. But there was no

170

one in the confessional line. We were alone. The Bishop was my friend, and my sins pleased him, and I could not deny him the joy of them.

"When I woke up, I felt no shame. None. Nada. I put on a new shirt, tucked it into my pants. I looked in the mirror to button down the shirt collar. I unbuttoned the pockets so that I could put things in them."

"Things."

"At K-Mart I stole a pack of gum and put it in my left pocket. At Walgreens I added a Parker pen and, for the other pocket, a comb. The kind with a plastic case. That is all," I said. "The End."

He said, "*Gracias.*" I pictured him happy. I pictured the cloud of freckles across his face, and sunlight shining through it. He told me his theory then, the first time he told me it. He had decided, he said, that the more you sin the closer you come to salvation. "The Bible tells this, Red. I never believed it." He gave examples. Mary Magdalene, the serial sinner. The Prodigal Son. Matthew, the tax collector. Peter, the triple denier. Red Greet, shirt stealer.

"I see," he said, "how you pray when you are planning to steal. Would you pray as much if you were pure? And would you watch for signs? And if you were sinless would you look into the mirror and see your soul, and baptize and martyr yourself?"

"It doesn't make sense," I said.

He said, "You're right. I'm working it out. I have to work on it."

"So?"

"So. It's a theory!"

"And will I ever be saved?" I asked.

"You are closer than most."

"And you?"

He turned on a light on his side of the confessional. "Me? I do not sin enough. It is a bishop's curse. Too few opportunities."

Through the window of our bedroom I hear humming: low, yearning sound, the way the owl sounds who can prophecy anything that will happen at night. Am I dreaming? "When an owl comes in a dream," my mother told me, "ask the owl about the darkness. If you can answer *who*, He will tell you the *what*, the *where*, and the *why*."

"Oh, Mother," I say, and push aside the sheets. But she has been dead for twenty years. I must be dreaming.

"Red, what is it?" asks Recita, who is in my dreams, of course, always has been.

I look through my closed eyes at my reflection in the window, then deeper in, and through, and out at last. Like looking at the moon through mulberry leaves. I ask, "Who is it?"

A boy.

A boy is trying to knock something out of the old mulberry tree of Otilia Félix. What is lodged there? He throws rocks and a baseball and empty tin soup cans and car tools and pieces of pipe at it to bring it down. He throws satin dancing slippers, white patent wedding shoes, and rolled newspapers, and soup spoons, and thin black socks, coats and jackets and wraps and cloaks and pictures of the saints and boxer shorts the color of marigolds. Some of the junk falls back to the ground. Some doesn't.

He hums.

He throws more rocks, his baseball again, his baseball glove and bat, a deflated soccer ball. He goes inside his house.

He comes back, dragging a trash bag almost as big as him. He empties it out. A box of crackers, half a dozen unopened cans of soup, hardback and paperback books, six or seven pairs of boys' and women's and men's shoes.

Whatever is lodged in the tree is not alone. Underneath whatever it is is a nest of junk the nestbuilder adds to. How will the boy play baseball now with his ball glove, bat, and cleats in the tree?

He hums to himself, the boy is humming sadly. You have heard this kind of humming. Can you ever forget if you have heard it? Hmmm. Hmmmmm.

Without knowing how I came to be there, I am with the boy. It is a dream, after all, and I believe I float down to him through the tree branches. He doesn't see me. His arms are small shelves full of books. Three hardbacks, two paperbacks spread their paper wings and fly up, and stay, and, there, that is what stories are worth. They add to the unanswered mystery or they knock it down.

Because he is humming that way, I do not ask, "What is up there that you want?"

I climb.

I can climb.

Old trees are for old men to climb. My bare, blessedly clean feet find a perch on her. My hands learn her as they go, and I keep my chest close to her trunk and my hips cantilevered so I am one slow but sure caterpillar. I am crying, my nose is watering. I have white boxer shorts on and nothing else. A jumbled question clots my heart, locking it closed. "Who you are?" it asks, and is thrown to every edge of my blood. For one instant I think I will shed the shorts in order to climb naked.

No. No.

I climb.

I am shining. I have been newly polished, and I am a shining man. I leave the shorts on.

What should I do? Where should I go? Why have I climbed the tree?

I ask the boy where it is.

No answer. I ask, "What is it?"

I climb out onto the neck of one of the limbs running through the nest of dreamjunk, and I know that this is what all the things we take and own and use and read and wear and lose are worth: a boy's misery nests in them.

A voice floats up through the boy's humming. "He will find it," the voice says, Recita's voice, dear Recita.

The voice sinks back everywhere inside me. Who you are? Who you are? A prayer I heard once from a child.

I will do this. I will be this. I will sit in the nest. Pink and shining and wet as a new caterpillar. As happily pointless as if the boy had flung me up here. If the nest will not hold me, I will die flying.

I hear my mother ask, "If I tell you, you will pray this?" From here, from this green island of dream, I see across the distances. There is my little altar, and there Eusebio's map dot, and there Gamboa's Restaurant, and the Hatch Chile Festival hangar and the chile fields, and Las Almas, and everywhere, everywhere, my father's walls, his rosaries of stone.

I see the boy in Recita's arms, but for a moment I imagine they are Cecilia's arms. I smell the perfume I rubbed into her hair, the oil the Bishop anointed her with, her eyes, ears, nostrils, lips. I taste the salty bread of the Blessed Sacrament. *Only say the word and I shall be healed.* I hear the passing-bell.

The boy is weeping because I will help now. Or weeping because I will fail. I creep along one bare limb. Red, red caterpillar, you are almost there, I say to myself.

Almost. Almost. Almost. And then.

I am there. There is a nest an angel might make, a round nest, amazing deep, round nest of kites, starched shirts, toga dresses, silver pieces, leather garden gloves, safety glasses, giant ledgers, compacts, lipsticks, radio books, bars of soap, hand-brushes, handballs, hand-tooled saddlebags, hand-carved tiaras, chocolate reindeer, and red bubble lights. Every twig and strand of hope I have ever known.

Now is the time, before I sit in that holy, secret place the boy has made over his own head, now is the time to ask the big question.

I ask, "What are you looking for?"

He is humming the way a hummingbird's wings hum, the way the blood of its sacred heart sings. That is all I hear: his humming. I ask, "What are you looking for?"

Quiet. The boy's humming suddenly stops. At the center of the nest I lie down. It is as dark as a confessional here. Bless me, Father. I've stolen from and hurt everyone I've ever loved and everyone who has ever believed in me and trusted and loved me. Bless me. I know I am forgiven. I know I am.

One last time, I ask the boy, "What are you looking for?"

"My hat," the boy says.

"How did it get up here?" I ask.

"I was happy."